WRITERS HARVEST 3

WRITERS HARVEST 3

EDITED AND
WITH AN
INTRODUCTION
BY

TOBIAS WOLFF

DELTA TRADE PAPERBACKS

A Delta Book
Published by
Dell Publishing
a division of
Random House, Inc.
1540 Broadway
New York, New York 10036

These short stories are works of fiction. Names, characters, places, and incidents either are the product of the author's imagination or are used fictitiously. Any resemblance to actual persons, living or dead, events, or locales is entirely coincidental.

Library of Congress Cataloging in Publication Data
Writers harvest 3 / edited and with an introduction by Tobias Wolff.
p. cm.
ISBN 0-385-33377-3
1. United States—Social life and customs—20th century—Fiction. 2. Short stories, American. I. Wolff, Tobias, 1945– . II. Title: Writers harvest three.
PS648.S5W76 2000
813'.0108054—dc21 99-33278
CIP

Design by Lynn Newmark

Manufactured in the United States of America
Published simultaneously in Canada

February 2000

10 9 8 7 6 5 4 3 2 1

BVG

CONTENTS

FOREWORD BY BILL SHORE vii

INTRODUCTION BY TOBIAS WOLFF ix

ANDRE DUBUS CORPORAL LEWIS 1

CHRIS OFFUTT OUT OF THE WOODS 5

JOHN BARTH EXTENSION 21

MARY GORDON THE BLIND NEIGHBOR 33

JASON BROWN AFTERNOON OF THE *SASSANOA* 49

FREDERICK BUSCH DEBRIEFNG 77

JACOB MOLYNEUX DESIRE LINES 95

TIM GAUTREAUX RODEO PATROL 113

JOYCE CAROL OATES THE PHOTOGRAPHER 119

THOMAS BELLER CALLER I.D. 131

BARRY LOPEZ STOLEN HORSES 145

JIM SHEPARD 'SCUSE ME, WHILE I KISS THIS GUY 153

BRIDGET ROHAN GARRITY THE HOLY BOYS 175

RALPH LOMBREGLIA CASHMERE CHRISTMAS 207

STEWART O'NAN 20 BURGERS 227

CONTRIBUTORS 253

FOREWORD

by Bill Shore

"Words signify man's refusal to accept the world as it is." This is what my eighth-grade English teacher, Mr. Klieger, scrawled on the blackboard on our first day of school. Though I cannot recall where the quote came from, its power has stayed with me since. We have raised $82 million to support antihunger and antipoverty efforts worldwide and have mobilized tens of thousands of individuals to contribute their own talents to such efforts since our founding in 1984. By supporting food assistance, treating malnutrition and other consequences of hunger, and promoting economic independence among people in need, SOS meets immediate demands for food while investing in long-term solutions to hunger and poverty. Others' words have played a significant role in our efforts to one day accept the world as a place without hunger.

Over the last eight years, writers have contributed their voices and words to this fight both by reading from their work at Writers Harvest: The National Reading events and by donating stories to anthologies such as this fine collection. Thanks to the incredibly talented fifteen writers who generously offered the best of themselves, we can now multiply our efforts. Their dedication to raising funds and awareness reflects what John Steinbeck wrote to his biographer: "As to the question as to what I mean by—or what my philosophy is—I haven't the least idea. And if I told you one, it wouldn't be true. I don't like people to be hurt or hungry or unnecessarily sad. It's just about as simple as that."

We also owe special thanks to Tobias Wolff, who chaired Writers Harvest: The National Reading in 1998, for dedicating countless hours to unite such talent to create this impressive collection of fiction. His commitment to helping others is an inspiration to all of us who are engaged in this work. The title of the national reading as well as the title of this, our third, Writers Harvest anthology remind me of a line from one of Gwendolyn Brooks's poems: "We are each other's harvest; we are each other's business; we are each other's magnitude and bond."

INTRODUCTION

Jack Yeats, the poet's father, once described writing as "the social act of a solitary man." This is a comforting idea, from a certain distance, and it has some truth on its side. Good work does something to its readers. Sometimes dramatically, more often subtly and slowly, it can change the way we see things, even the way we behave. But the actual experience of writing does not feel like a social act; it feels like the solitary act of a solitary person.

Solitude is the very condition of writing. You can't do it with other people around unless you forget they're there, which means that for practical purposes they're *not* there. To write, you must concentrate, concentrate long and hard, and being alone is the price of that concentration. It takes years of self-imposed quarantine to write even a bad novel.

We accept this, however grudgingly. But even those of us who cherish our solitude can't help but worry that the long practice of it will isolate us from the common run of life, where social acts have more frequent and visible results.

Most writers are interested in what happens to the people outside their stories. And if they're interested, they have to ask themselves what their work—which proceeds from the luxury of unencumbered time—has to do with the desperate lives of just about everybody else in the world. Forget the world; in this country alone, this richest of all the countries that ever were, many millions of people are hungry as I write these words. A disproportionate number of them are kids. Hungry children make poor students; they can't concentrate—concentration itself is a luxury of the well-fed. Hungry children lose ground fast, and even if they do get the food they need later on, the physiological and emotional damage they've already suffered makes it unlikely they'll ever catch up. Even the most self-interested of us must cringe at the notion of all these children coming of age without the knowledge or skills to take their place in a society based on competition. If they can't join us, what, then, will they do? How will they control the rage they must feel at being left to their hunger while the rest of us grew fat on the land?

Writers give money, they work in food pantries, they do what other people do who wear their ease uneasily. But a question remains: Writing alone, and most often on subjects that don't directly confront the scandal of our neighbors' hunger, how can we make our work part of the struggle against it?

I am grateful to Share Our Strength for giving us at least a couple of ways. On a given October day for several years now, SOS has sponsored benefit readings all over the country at which thousands of writers come together to share their stories and poems. The money raised at these events is distributed to food banks and homeless shelters, wherever the need is greatest. Toward the same end, SOS has made it possible for writers to contribute their work to anthologies like this one, all profits to go for the relief of hunger. Through these and similar efforts, including pro bono culinary extravaganzas staged by chefs and caterers and restaurateurs, SOS has raised many millions of dollars over the last fifteen years.

What a simple, beautiful idea—to allow artists the chance to put their work at the service of others without any sanctimonious distortions of their voices and interests. Though the writers in these pages are doing good work, there is no sign of any intention to commit Good Works. It's a remarkably varied gathering: writers just beginning their lives in print, others with shelves of books to their credit; stories that warm the old pump, stories that freeze the veins; language salty and tough as jerky or ripe and warm as a pear just lifted from the windowsill. These stories have only this in common: All are gifts. It has been nothing but a pleasure to receive them, and now I have the even greater pleasure of passing them on to you.

—Tobias Wolff

ANDRE
DUBUS

CORPORAL LEWIS

At four-thirty on a summer day in California, the marine captain left the barracks and drove past hills to the Officers' Club and, at the bar, found his friend, also a captain, among men and women in uniform sitting and standing. The bar was brightly lit. He ordered a martini and said: "Today I lost a man, to the hospital in Philadelphia. A good corporal. He said God was talking to him."

"Out loud?"

"Yes. Something kicked it off. He was at a bar last night with some marines. He didn't like the way his buddies were talking to the waitress. He told them they should stop. I talked to a corporal who was there. He said Lewis seemed sad."

"When did God start talking?"

"This morning. Then he walked around the barracks

saying God told him to tell people they should be kind to one another. The platoon sergeant talked to him, then brought him to the platoon commander. He talked to him; the XO's on leave, so the lieutenant came to me and said Lewis was having some kind of breakdown, so I said to send him in. The S-three called. It was eleven forty-five. Lewis came in and went to the radiator at the window. He kneeled there and looked outside. The S-three finally stopped talking and Lewis was still kneeling and staring. So I went over there. I said: 'Lewis. Are you all right?' He said: 'Yes, sir.' He was staring at the sun. He wasn't blinking. I looked at the sun. Blink blink blink. Then he said: 'God told me to tell people to be kind.' "

The bartender brought the captain his martini, and a second for his friend, who sipped and said: "Schizophrenic."

"Or something. I'm a Catholic, I grew up with these stories, Joan of Arc, Moses, Saint Paul, on and on. I believe them. But this was in my office, and it was spooky. I felt like there was something else in the room with us. I called the S-one and took Lewis to battalion. We walked on the road. He got in step with me. I said: 'Can you hear God?' He said: 'Sometimes, sir.' I said: 'Since when?' He said: 'Since chow line this morning.' I said: 'Are you hearing Him now?' He said: 'No, sir; only you and me.' We went to the colonel and I told him and he called the doctor, and told us to sit down. He asked Lewis if he'd ever heard voices before. Lewis said: 'No, sir.' The colonel passed his cigarettes around. He paced behind his desk. He said:

'We'll take care of you, son.' I watched the side of Lewis's face. He looked the same as he did eight months ago, when he joined the company. The doctor and two corpsmen came and I shook Lewis's hand, told him he'd be fine. He said: 'Yes, sir, I will be.' He looked peaceful. The colonel patted his shoulder. They're flying him out tonight. But I wonder something. What if I hadn't done anything? Just brought him to the field tomorrow, for platoon tactics. And what if he'd done his job? What would that mean? You asked when God started talking to him. I'm wondering when He stopped talking to people. You think a Cheyenne warrior would have had a problem with Lewis?"

"Not if he was on their side."

"Nothing he said was crazy."

"It's how he said it. And hearing God."

"There's something else. He was squared away, spit and polish, he could have passed inspection by a martinet. He cared about the waitress. He looked at the sun and it didn't hurt his eyes."

CHRIS
OFFUTT

OUT OF THE WOODS

Gerald opened his front door at dawn, wearing only a quickly drawn-on pair of jeans. His wife's four brothers stood in the ground fog that filtered along the ridge. The oldest brother had become family spokesman after the father's death, and Gerald waited for him to speak. The mother was still boss, but everything had to filter through a man.

"It's Ory," the oldest one said. "He got shot and is in the hospital. Somebody's got to fetch him."

The brothers looked at Gerald from below their eyebrows. Going after Ory wasn't a chore anyone wanted, and Gerald was new to the family, married to Kay, the only sister. He still needed to prove his worth. If he brought Ory home, maybe they'd cut the barrier that kept him on the edge of things, like he was nothing but a third or fourth cousin.

"Where's he at?" Gerald said.

"Wahoo, Nebraska. Ory said it would take two days but was easy to find."

"My rig won't make it."

"You can take the old Ford. She'll run till doomsday."

"Who shot him?"

The oldest brother flashed him a mean look. The rest were back to looking down, as if they were carpenters gauging the amount of linoleum needed for a job.

"Some woman," the oldest brother said.

Kay began to cry. The brothers left and Gerald sat on the couch beside Kay. She hugged her knees and bit a thumbnail, gasping in a throaty way that reminded him of the sounds she made in bed. He reached for her. She shrugged from his hand, then allowed his touch.

"Him leaving never made sense," Kay said. "He hadn't done nothing and nobody was after him. He didn't tell a soul why. Just up and went. Be ten years come fall."

"I'll go get him," he whispered.

"You don't care to?"

"No."

"For my brother?"

"For you."

She snuggled against him, her damp face pressed to his neck. She was tiny inside the robe. He opened the front and she pushed against his leg.

The next day he left in the black pickup. Gerald was

thirty years old and had never been out of the county. He wore a suit that was snug in the shoulders, and short in the legs. It had belonged to his father, but he didn't figure anyone would notice. He wished he owned a tie. The dogwoods and redbuds had already lost their spring color. The air was hot. In four hours he was in Indiana, where the land was flat as a playing card. There was nowhere to hide, no safety at all. Even the sun was too bright. He didn't understand how Ory could stand such open ground.

Illinois was equally flat but with less green to it. Gerald realized that he was driving through a season, watching spring in reverse. The Illinois dirt was black as manure and he pulled over to examine it. The earth was moist and rich. It smelled of life. He let it trickle between his fingers, thinking of the hard clay dirt at home. He decided to stop and get some of this good dirt on the way back.

He drove all day and into the night, and covered most of Iowa. At a rest area he unrolled a blanket and lay down. He was cold. Above him the stars were strewn across the sky. They seemed to be moving down, threatening to press him against the ground. Something bright cut across the night, and he thought someone had shot at him until he realized it was a shooting star. The hills at home blocked so much sky that he'd never seen one. He watched the vast prairie night until fading into sleep.

The eerie light of a flatland dawn woke him early. The sun wasn't visible and the world seemed to glow from within. There were no birds to hear. He could see his breath. He drove west and left the interstate at Wahoo and found the hospital easily. A nurse took him to a small room. Everything was white and the walls seemed to emit a low hum. He couldn't place the smell. A man came into the room wearing a white coat. He spoke with an accent.

"I am Dr. Gupte. You are with the family of Mr. Gordon?"

"You're the doctor?"

"Yes." He sighed and opened a manila folder. "I'm afraid Mr. Gordon has left us."

"Done out, huh. Where to?"

"I'm afraid that is not the circumstance."

"It's not."

"No, he had a pulmonary thromboembolism."

"Is that American?"

"I'm afraid you will excuse me."

Dr. Gupte left the room and Gerald wondered who the funny little man really was. He pulled open a drawer. Inside was a small mallet with a triangular head made of soft rubber, perfect for nothing. A cop came in the room, and Gerald slowly closed the drawer.

"I'm Sheriff Tunis. You the next of kin?"

"Gerald Caudill."

They watched each other in the tiny room under the artificial light. Gerald didn't like cops. They got to carry a gun, drive fast, and fight. Anybody else got thrown in the pokey for doing the same thing.

"Dr. Gupte asked me to come in," the sheriff said.

"He really is a doctor?"

"He's from Pakistan."

"Run out of your own, huh?"

"Look, Mr. Caudill. Your brother-in-law got a blood clot that went to his lung. He died from it."

Gerald cleared his throat, scanned the floor for somewhere to spit, then swallowed it. He rubbed his eyes.

"Say he's dead."

The sheriff nodded.

"That damn doctor ain't worth his hide, is he?"

"It wasn't his fault."

"Shoot, I drove two days straight."

"There's some things to clear up."

The sheriff drove Gerald to his office, a small space with a desk and two chairs. A calendar hung from the wall. The room reminded Gerald of the hospital without the smell.

"Ory was on a tear," the sheriff said. "He was drinking and wrecked his car at his girlfriend's house. She wouldn't let him in and he broke the door open. They started arguing and she shot him."

"And he got the blood clot."

The sheriff nodded.

"Did he not have a job?"

"No. And there's some money problems. He went through a fence and hit a light post. He owed back rent at a rooming house. Plus the hospital."

"Car bad hurt?"

"It runs."

"Did he own anything?"

"Clothes, a knife, suitcase, a little twenty-two pistol, a pair of boots, and a radio."

"What all does he owe?"

"Twelve hundred dollars."

Gerald walked to the window. He thought of his wife and all her family waiting for him. Gerald didn't know what to do, but he damn sure wasn't going to call home. The family had given him a little money, but he'd need it for gas on the ride back.

"Can I see her?" he said.

"Who?"

"That woman that shot him."

The sheriff led him across the street to a tan building made of stone. Near the eaves were narrow slits to let light in. They went through heavy doors into a common room with a TV set and a pay phone. Four cells formed one wall. A woman sat on a bunk in one of the cells, reading a magazine. She wore an orange jumpsuit that was too big for her.

"Melanie," the sheriff said. "You have a visitor. Ory's brother-in-law."

The sheriff left and Gerald stared through the bars. Her hair was dark purple. One side was long, the other shaved. Each ear had several small gold hoops in a row that reminded Gerald of a guide for a harness. A gold ring pierced her left nostril. She had a black eye. He wanted to watch her for a long time, but looked at his boots instead.

"Hidy," he said.

She rolled the magazine into a tube and held it to her good eye, looking at Gerald.

"I come to get Ory, but he's died on me. Just thought I'd talk to you a minute."

"I didn't kill him."

"I know it."

"I only shot him."

"It was a blood clot killed him."

"Do you want to screw me?"

Gerald shook his head, his face turning red. She seemed too young to talk that way, too young for jail, too young for Ory.

"Let me have a cigarette," she said.

He passed one through the bars and she took it without touching his hand. A chain was tattooed around her wrist. She French-inhaled, pulling twin lines of smoke from her mouth into her nose. The ash was long and red. She sucked at the filter, lifting her lips to prevent them from getting burned. She blew a smoke ring. Gerald had never seen anyone get so much out of one cigarette.

"Wish it was menthol," she said. "Ory smoked menthol."

"Well."

"What do you want?" she said.

"I don't know. Nothing, I don't guess."

"Me, neither, except out of here."

"Don't reckon I can help you there."

"You talk just like Ory did."

"How come you to shoot him?"

"We had a fight, and he like, came over drunk. He

wanted something he gave me and I wouldn't give it back. It was mine. He busted the lock and started tearing everything up, you know, looking for it. I had a little pistol in my vanity and I like, got it out."

Melanie finished the cigarette and he gave her another one, careful not to look at the ring in her nose. Behind her was a stainless steel toilet with a sink on top where the tank should be. When you washed your hands, it flushed the toilet. He thought of the jail at home with its putrid hole in the floor and no sink at all.

"What was it he was wanting so bad?"

"A wig," she said. "It was blond and he liked me to wear it. Sometimes I wore it in bed."

"You shot him over a wig."

"I was scared. He kept screaming, 'Give me back my wig.' So I, you know, shot him. Just once. If I knew he'd get that blood clot, I wouldn't have done it."

Gerald wondered how old she was but didn't want to insult her by asking. He felt sorry for her.

"He give you that eye?"

"The cops did. They think me and Ory sell dope but we don't, not really. Nothing heavy. Just to like, friends."

"Why do you do that?" he said.

"Deal?"

"No. Cut your hair and stick that thing in your nose."

"Shut up," she said. She began yelling. "I don't need you. Get away from me. Get out of here!"

The sheriff came into the common room and took Gerald outside. The sky was dark with the smell of rain. He wanted to stand there until the storm swept over him, rinsing him of the jail. He underwent a sudden sense of vertigo, and for a moment he didn't know where he was, only that he was two days from anything familiar. He didn't even know where his truck was.

"She's a hard one," the sheriff said.

"I don't want no charges pressed against her."

"That's not up to you."

"She didn't kill him."

"I don't know about Kentucky," the sherrif said, "but in Nebraska, shooting people's a crime. Look, there's been a big wreck on Ninety-two and five people are coming to the hospital. They need the space. We got to get your brother-in-law to a funeral home."

"Can't afford it."

"The hospital's worse. It charges by the day."

"What in case I take his stuff and leave?"

"The county'll bury him."

"That'll run you how much?"

"About a thousand."

"That's a lot of money."

The sheriff nodded.

"Tell you what," Gerald said. "I'll sell you his car for one dollar. You can use it to pay off what all he owes. Plus there's that radio and stuff."

"That won't be near enough."

"I'll throw in a hundred cash."

"You can't buy a body."

"It ain't yours to sell or mine to buy. I just want to get him home. Family wants him."

"I don't know if it's legal."

"He ain't the first person to die somewhere else. My cousin's aunt came in on a train after getting killed in a wreck. They set her off at the station in Rocksalt. She was in a box."

The sheriff puffed his cheeks and blew air. He went to his office and dialed the courthouse and asked for a notary public. Half an hour later the car belonged to the city of Wahoo. It was a Chevelle and for a moment Gerald wondered if he'd made a mistake.

The sheriff drove them to the hospital. Gerald pulled the money out and started counting.

"Keep it," the sheriff said.

"Give it to Melanie. She wants menthol cigarettes."

"You and Ory aren't a whole lot alike, are you?"

"I never knew him that good."

"The only man I saw give money away was my daddy."

"Was he rich?"

"No," said the sheriff, "Daddy was a farmer."

"You all worked this flat land?"

"It worked him right back into it."

Gerald followed the sheriff into the hospital and signed several forms. An orderly wheeled in a gurney with the body on it, covered with a white cloth. He pushed it to an exit beside the emergency room. Three ambulances came into the lot and paramedics began moving the injured people into the hospital. The orderlies left the gurney and went to help. A state police car stopped behind the ambulances.

"I have to talk to them," the sheriff said. "Then I'll get an ambulance to drop the body down at the train station."

Gerald nodded, as the sheriff left. Nobody was looking at Gerald. He pushed the gurney into the lot and along the side of the building. A breeze rippled the cloth that covered Ory. Gerald held it down with one hand but the gurney went crooked. He let go of the cloth and righted the gurney and the wind blew the cloth away. Ory was stretched out naked with a hole in his side. He didn't look dead, but Gerald didn't think he looked too good either. He looked like a man with a bad hangover that he could shake by the end of the day.

Gerald dropped the tailgate of his pickup and dragged Ory into the truck. He threw his blanket over him and weighted the corners with tire tools, the spare, and a coal shovel. Outside of town he tied the blanket down with wire and hay string, and drove the rest of the day. In Illinois he stopped and lay down beside the truck. Without the blanket he was cold, but he didn't feel right about taking it back from Ory. Gerald thought about the blond wig, how Ory had asked Melanie to wear it. He wondered if it made a difference when they were in bed.

He woke with frost on him. A buzzard circled high above the truck. He drove into the rising sun, thinking that he'd done everything backward. No matter when he drove, he was always aimed at the sun. Mist lifted above the land as the frost gave way. At the next exit Gerald left the interstate for a farm road and parked beneath a cottonwood beside a plowed field.

He carried the shovel over a wire fence to the field. The dirt was loose and easy to take. It would make a fine garden at home. His body took over, grateful for the labor after three days of driving. A pair of redwing blackbirds sat on a power line, courting each other. Gerald wondered how birds knew to go with their own kind. Maybe Ory knew he was in the wrong tree and that's why he wanted Melanie to wear a wig. Gerald tried to imagine her with blond hair. He suddenly understood that he wanted her, had wanted her at the jailhouse. He couldn't figure why. It bothered him that he had so much desire for a woman he didn't consider attractive. He wondered if she liked his suit.

He climbed in the back to balance the load, mounding the dirt in the middle. As he traveled south, he reentered spring. The buds of softwood trees turned pale green. Flocks of starlings moved over him in a dark cloud, heading north. By nightfall he crossed the Ohio river into Kentucky. In four hours he'd be home. He was getting sleepy, but coffee had stopped doing him any good. He slid into a zone of the road, letting the rhythm of motion enter his body. A loud noise made him jerk upright. He thought he'd had a flat until he saw that he'd drifted across the breakdown lane and onto the edge of the median. He parked and lay down in the bench seat. He was lucky not to have been killed. The law would have a hard time with that—two dead men, one naked and already stiff, and a load of dirt.

When he woke, it was light and he felt tired already. At a gas station he stared at the rest-room mirror, thinking that he looked like the third day of a three-day drunk. The suit was ruined. He combed his hair with water and stepped into the sun. A dog was in the back of his pickup, digging. Gerald yelled, looking for something to grab. The dog saw him and jumped off the truck and loped away. Gerald shoved dirt over Ory's exposed hand. A man came behind him.

"Shoo-eee," the man said. "You waited long enough didn't you?"

Gerald grunted. He was smoothing the dirt, replacing the weights along the blanket's edge. The man spoke again.

"Had to take one to the renderers myself last week. Got some kind of bug that killed it in three days. Vet said it was a new one on him."

"A new one."

"I put mine in a garbage bag. Keeps the smell in better than dirt."

"It does."

"Did yours up and not eat, then lay down and start breathing hard?"

"More or less."

"It's the same thing. A malady, the vet called it."

"A malady."

Gerald got in the truck and decided not to stop until he was home. The stench was bad and getting worse. He wondered if breathing a bad smell made your lungs stink. The land started to roll, the crests rising higher as he traveled east. The sun was very hot. It seemed to him as if summer had arrived while he was gone. He'd been to winter and back.

Deep in the hills he left the interstate for a blacktop road that turned to dirt, following the twists of a creek. He stopped at the foot of his wife's home hill. Kay would be up there, at her mom's house with all her family. They would feed him, give him whiskey, wait for him to tell what happened. He brushed off his suit and thought about the events, collecting them in sequence. He told the story in his head. He thought some more, then practiced it again. Ory had quit drinking and had a good job as manager of a department store. He'd gotten engaged to a woman he'd met at church, but had held off telling the family until he could bring her home. She was nice as pie, blond headed. He was teaching her to shoot a pistol and it went off by accident. She was tore all to pieces about it. He'd never seen anyone in such bad shape. All she did was cry. It was a malady.

Gerald drove slowly up the hill. Later, he could tell the truth to the oldest brother, who'd tell the rest. They'd appreciate his public lie and he'd be one in with the family. He parked in the yard beside his mother-in-law's house. Dogs ran toward the truck, then kids. Adults stepped onto the porch and Gerald could see them looking for Ory in the cab. Kay came out of the house. She smiled at him, the same small smile that she always used, and he wondered how she'd look in a wig.

He got out of the truck and waited. Everything was the same—the house, the trees, the people. He recognized the leaves and the outline of the branches against the sky. He knew how the light would fall, where the shadows would go. The smell of the woods was familiar. It would be this way forever. Abruptly, as if doused by water, he knew why Ory had left.

JOHN

BARTH

EXTENSION

Two quick decades later, in the assisted living facility, I hear him telling the story this way, perhaps to himself:

"The little project seemed on the face of it desirable, feasible, even natural. We would enlarge and reequip my home office (Myrna found hers adequate as it was), together with our bedroom and the bath connecting them. Contiguous to that master bedroom and the long screened porch we would add a solarium/spa/exercise room to help us stay fit in our approaching retirement: all this in an integrated, architecturally pleasing extension to our modest rural hideaway overlooking a tidal creek and the broad river beyond it—itself a tributary of the bay and, by extension, of the Atlantic and thence all other oceans. In one's elder years, Myrna liked to joke, it's important to remain in touch with the world.

"Granted, this proposed extension was more ambitious than a number of our earlier, trial-run improvements to what we had bought, some dozen years before, as a weekend retreat and vacation house. An unremarkable but adequate and nicely situated 1950s-style 'rancher,' it was replete with Eisenhower-era picture windows, fake shutters, brick-veneer siding, stock asphalt roof-shingles, barebones landscaping. The place was meant to supplement our equally modest, okay-for-its-purposes house in the city, convenient to our main offices; over the years of our parttime residency we had white-painted the bricks, replaced the Thermopane picture windows with divided-pane bays, redecked the pier, added a freshwater pool to complement the saltwater creek, relandscaped the lot, remodeled the kitchen and the guest accommodations, upgraded the heating, air-conditioning, and water systems, installed overhead paddle-fans, skylights, and privacy fencing, and replaced the roof, as well as making less extensive improvements in our town house—older, but better built and less in need of upgrading. Our His-and-Her counseling careers (investment and marriage, respectively) had gone well, as had our lives in general; we were comfortably off. I myself happened to be of just the right age to have missed all the wars of our horrific century—not here for the First World War, too young for the Second, student-deferred from Korea, too old for Vietnam—and to have prospered in the post-WWII economy; nothing worse had thus far befallen the pair of us than the breakup of our respective first marriages (pains more than assuaged by our successful second, with its live-in counselor), the loss of aged parents, the occasional illness, injury, or child-raising crisis, and other such less-than-mortal shocks. If this house-extension project was more considerable than its forerunners, it was less so than numerous other of our major life-moves: the engenderment of children, the several changes of job-and-living-venues that are par for the American professional course, the divorces and remarriage aforementioned, the purchase and furnishing of those two houses and their predecessors. Not only did our economic position and life-situation make the proposed extension appear unremarkable (up and down the estuary one saw more ambitious projects in progress); it was itself just another extension both of our personal joint history and of our American generation's—indeed, of our American Century's. Over the hundred-odd years since our respective grandparents had immigrated, each crop of their descendants (until our own baby-boom children, anyhow) had on average grown taller, more prosperous, and longer lived than its forebears. Like most of our middle-class compatriots, we ourselves had grown not just bodily from infancy through childhood to maturity but likewise (and thus far lifelong) in our physical, mental, and spiritual capacities, our skills and responsibilities, our professional status, authority, and earning power—and, along with those (as the Dow Jones rose from the five hundreds to the five-plus thousands, and the American divorce rate climbed with it), in the number, size, and quality of our material possessions and accommodations. From Spartan student lodgings Myrna and I had 'moved up,' separately and together, through entry-level apartments and secondhand automobiles to our first new cars and minimal homeownerships; from one child to two, one car to two (one marriage to two, I'm tempted to add), one house to two plus a small boat, *two* small boats, two less-small boats plus more-expensive cars and houses plus more frequent and less frugal vacation trips plus that swimming pool and paid-off mortgages and country-club memberships and ever-growing equity accounts and 'starter' trust funds for the grandchildren and those several initiatory remodelings and property improvements aforementioned—all leading almost logically, one might say, to this latest, really not extraordinary extension-in-the-works.

"Did we *need* it? Well: Does one 'need' a larger sportfishing cruiser, a better-made car, a more extensive (and expensive) vacation? We *wanted* it; we *could use* it; we had, in our opinion, *earned* it. It would be yet another 'improvement,' another . . . *extension*, in a word, of our life-estate as well as of our (Number Two) house—an extension the more desirable for its being, not impossibly, our last such. We were, as aforeremarked, approaching the traditional American retirement age, and although we enjoyed our professions and had by no means decided to quit them entirely, it had in fact been some years already since we'd last *increased* our separate counseling responsibilities. Indeed, we had not only leveled off on that particular front but cut back a bit (in my case particularly, as I was the elder of us and less in need of an outside office): fewer and less extended business trips, shorter working hours, longer and more frequent vacations, fewer days per week and month and year in the city place, and more in the country. Did we need the extension? With our children out of the nest and raising nestlings of their own in distant cities, we didn't really 'need' the residential square-footage that we occupied already, enough to house half a dozen ghetto or Third World families. But we were neither of those, and particularly given this recent gradual shift of our domestic gravity-center from city to country, the proposed extension seemed, as aforedeclared, both desirable and feasible. It was not, after all, another or newer or bigger-and-better *house,* as might have been the case ten years before. It was simply . . . an extension.

"And so we made preliminary measurements and sketches; with some misgivings we reengaged the architect who had 'done' our trial-run projects; we studied and annotated and conferred upon and revised her more extensive drawings and specifications; over the following year-and-then-some, as we went about our businesses and pleasures, we bethought ourselves and more than once rethought the design, even the whole project. I say 'with some misgivings' because those earlier remodelings had by no means been hassle free. When were such things ever? There were the usual (perhaps rather more than the usual) unforeseen problems, cost overruns, delays, compromises. With the results we were, on the whole, quite pleased, though perhaps mainly relieved to have the several little ordeals behind us and still unhappy with certain features of the jobs—those if-we-were-doing-it-again things that we continued to believe a better architect would have anticipated, or a more knowledgeable builder warned us of. And so rather than bolstering our confidence in those professionals and in ourselves, the trial runs had proved ambivalent trials indeed. To shift designers now, however, would have been to turn this more considerable project into another trial run, when as far as we could see (and had by now come rather to hope), nothing in the 'extension' way lay beyond it. Life is not a dress rehearsal, declares the bumper sticker; Better the devil you know than the devil you don't, advises the proverb. All the same, we felt less prepared for the Main Event than we had expected to feel when its time came. Thus our misgivings.

"But the calendar was running. As seasons passed, we found ourselves more and more merely maintaining the town house while chafing at the limitations of what after all we had never intended as our primary residence. And so we came to put ever more time, energy, and money into planning that capital-E Extension, as we now thought of it. On corkboards in our home offices we pinned volumetric drawings of the remodeled country-seat-cum-extension, to encourage and inspire us in odd moments. Perhaps because those drawings were thus always before us, we further altered several major features of the design, as well as countless details. Every one of those alterations, needless to say, added slightly or substantially to the architect's fees, already so much higher than we had anticipated that we half-seriously wondered whether her 'trial-run' bills had been bait to hook us with. Like lawyers and some other sorts of counselors (myself and Myrna not excluded), hourly-rate designers thrive on complications and changes of plan; while we hemmed and hawed and revised and unrevised, her meter profitably ran. We had expected to have our extension built, decorated, furnished, landscaped, and ready for occupancy by retirement time, but when at last we declared the blueprints final (no doubt partly from fatigue, although every one of our many modifications and nearly every one of hers had been an improvement) and put the project out for bids, the several contractors' estimates came in so startlingly above even our architect's guesstimations that—frustrated, chagrined, and weary of the whole business—we put the project on Hold for a year in order to recollect ourselves, recounsel, reconsider. We shifted furniture to make more efficient use of our present space, ran in extra fax and computer-modem lines, did some much-needed temporary landscaping of the area that the Extension had been meant to cover, and promised ourselves not to think further about the thing for a full twelve months. Although the drawings remained in place on our corkboards, other matters duly distracted us: passing illnesses, pleasure travel upon those interconnected oceans and the continents they separate, problems large and small in the extended family, further drawdown of our professional activities, financial planning for our retirement—in all, a welcome return to normalcy.

"The turning point, I see now, was not our year-long moratorium but our discovery—when in an eyeblink that year passed and we duly fetched out for reinspection the sheaf of blueprints and specifications labeled EXTENSION—that we had come to feel we didn't really 'need' (you understand my meaning) quite so *much* extra space—although if we could have had it simply by snapping our fingers and paying the bills, we would have done so unhesitatingly. Why not scale the project down a bit, we asked ourselves—perhaps rather a lot? Halve the size of A, for example, while going forward with B as originally planned but dropping C entirely? The idea seemed feasible enough to warrant our reopening, no more eagerly than before, the connection with our architect; she cheerfully redrafted our scaled-down plan (to which we ourselves had devoted days, in hope of scaling down her fees as well) and billed us therefor. Ironically, however, we found our enthusiasm comparably reduced. Now that the country place had become in effect our main residence, the prospect of camping in half of it for several months while the other half was being noisily and messily extended seemed more disagreeable than ever, especially given a scaled-down payoff at the end. Moreover, in the period of our moratorium we had installed a spa on the barbecue patio beside the screened porch, a somewhat crowded but on the whole satisfactory substitute for the exercise room deleted from our scaled-down plan. And that 'temporary' landscaping had settled in and begun to grow handsomely; and we had begun seriously to consider selling the little city house when our professional phaseout was complete—all the more reason to enlarge the country place, we supposed, yet all the more daunting a prospect to do so, as the town house itself by this time needed substantial sprucing up if it was going to move in what had lately become a buyers' market.

"And so we dallied, counseled our respective (and reduced) clienteles, did other things—and noticed, for the first time, really, that doing them took longer than it used to. November was upon us before October's chores were done; how had we ever managed them when both of us were working full-time, not to mention when we were raising children too? A day came when—in process of shifting further items from our 'main house,' now for sale, to our 'weekend house,' now unequivocally our headquarters—we took down from our corkboards those aging volumetric sketches (which anyhow depicted the original, larger Extension, not its scaled-down succedanea) and filed them away with the so-costly blueprints, spec sheets, light-fixture catalogs, builders' proposals, and related correspondence. We told each other that when the convulsions of selling the town house and reordering our life were behind us, we might very well come back to the project. To ourselves, however, we acknowledged (at least one of us did) that we almost certainly would *not* come back to it; that our time for ambitious extensions had passed.

"Indeed (we came to see but not necessarily to say) the contrary had quietly become the case: for us, the order of the season and no doubt of all seasons to come was not extension but contraction. Just as we no longer needed two houses, so we no longer really needed two cars, far less a virtual flotilla of assorted watercraft. Why we continued to maintain separate home offices, even, except as personal retreats, had become a reasonable question, now that neither of us was really 'working.' One house (unextended), one car, one boat (small), would surely do: with our children scattered to the four winds and their parents gray haired, who waterskied any longer behind our aging outboard runabout? When had we or any guest last used our much-weathered canoe? Soon enough we would scarcely 'need' even our dear old flagship, so laborious for us to maintain and so expensive to hire the maintenance of; soon enough we would doubtless come to wish that our single, too-large house were a carefree condominium somewhere, so that we'd have more time to spend with our far-flung offspring and to explore further the world's interconnections while we were still able—except that traveling had lately become as much a chore as an adventure, and our relations with those offspring, while certainly affectionate, were inevitably attenuated by distance and by their own divorce/remarriages. Even visiting nearer-by family and friends, not to mention entertaining them at home, we found yearly more burdensome.

"They say that the universe itself is extending, extending; seems to me the case could be made that for some time now it's been holding still at best, while we ourselves have begun to shrink. Time was when the pair of us each worked a job and a half, raised kids and pets and vegetables and flowers, cooked and sewed and housecleaned, maintained scrupulously our houses and grounds and cars and boats, even did much of our own carpentry and plumbing and electrical repairs, and somehow still had time and energy left over for hobbies, sports, community activities, hospitality, good works. Lately it's enough to keep ourselves respectably dressed, groomed, fed. Who would have imagined that so trifling a matter as taking down a drawing from a corkboard could discover the Abyss? That in the mere canceling of a proposed house-extension one would feel brushed by the Dark Angel's wingfeathertips? Yet here we sit, Myrna and I, at our lorn bay window like ticketed passengers in an airport lounge, looking dully about us at the scene we're about to leave, waiting for the boarding call, for the ultimate contraction."

MARY GORDON

THE BLIND NEIGHBOR

Ellie was good about asking when she needed help. Probably she'd always known she couldn't get along without help, or anyway that was what I guessed made her so natural. She didn't apologize, she didn't put you in the bad position of pretending you had a choice—let's face it, there was no choice about helping a blind neighbor when she asked you. But she didn't make you feel resentful or like you were trapped, or at least she never made me feel that way. Maybe it was because she was so good-looking.

Of course there's no reason why a blind person shouldn't be good-looking. I mean, just because they can't see themselves it doesn't mean—what do I mean? I mean that the word *look* does have a double meaning. Like those dirty words, or those half dirty words. "That has a double meaning," people say, and the other meaning is always dirty. Because after all, you can be good-looking if you can't look. Or see. But if you can't see you can't look, can you? Or can't you? The words play tricks with you. With Ellie, sometimes I'd get embarrassed if I said, "I see," or "you see." Sometimes I'd stop in the middle of a sentence, that's how mortified I was. But Ellie would only laugh. "Oh, Ronald, you're such a literalist," she said once. I remembered the word *literalist.* "Blind people can't afford to be that literal."

I never did know why she always seemed so well dressed. I wondered if someone picked her clothes out for her. I guess they must have. The colors at least.

And she had that wonderful hair. It made me sad that she couldn't appreciate her own hair. Or maybe she could in some ways. I think she liked the texture of it. Maybe the weight.

I wondered if she knew she was good-looking and her husband wasn't. I wondered if he knew she was good-looking. It would be different for him than for her. She was born blind; he'd gone blind as an adult. I don't know how, I didn't like to ask. So he would have some memory or know the difference between good-looking and bad-looking. Or good-looking and whatever the opposite is. Un–good-looking. Plain. But what could the whole business mean to them? I was very curious about it, but I knew I could never ask her. Sometimes I thought if we got to be really good friends I could ask her someday. But that won't happen now.

* * *

She, or I should say, they, moved into my building at the end of August the year before last. So it was a year and a half ago that I first met her. Or them.

I saw her first from the back. The first thing I saw about her was her hair, that really unusual shade of red, so deep there seemed to be some royal blue or midnight blue or some very dark blue mixed in it. Seeing her from the back—she was just standing by the elevator with her dog—I couldn't tell that she was blind. I guess I should have been able to tell from the dog's harness. Ordinary dogs don't have that kind of harness. But I didn't pick that up. I just noticed the hair. And I said to myself that she had a nice figure from the back. What I said to myself was "She has a nice ass." But that's not the kind of thing I like to think of myself saying. Nevertheless, those are the words that came. But even then I noticed she had poor posture. I suppose that was another clue. But as I said, I wasn't picking up clues too well because all my attention was on her hair.

I walked up and pressed the elevator button, one of those stupid things people do even when the button's lit up, you can see it's already been pressed. But I didn't want to seem like I was staring. Now I know that wasn't really a consideration. But I didn't at the time. That's not completely right, though. It would have been a consideration. She would have sensed my presence. "I have a very strong sense of people's presence" was something she often said.

* * *

I introduced myself and told her my apartment number. I said if there was anything she needed she should just buzz. She said, "But I don't even know your name."

"Ronald," I said. "Like Ronald Colman."

I forgot how young she was, that the name Ronald Colman wouldn't mean anything to her. But I'd be damned if, as a lifelong Democrat, I was going to say, "Like Ronald Reagan." I didn't have to say anything. The name isn't that unusual.

"I'm Ellie," she said.

But wait, I'm skipping ahead. I'm skipping over the part when I found out she was blind. Because she was wearing sunglasses at first, and I still wasn't picking up the clue of the dog's harness. *The Clue of the Dog's Harness.* It sounds like one of those English mysteries. Ellie liked to listen to mysteries on tape. I bought her some in one of those new bookstores. Huge. I had to take an escalator two flights up to the "Recorded Word" section. I tried to keep an eye out for things that she might like. Since I'm retired, I have time on my hands. I was a CPA. I did her and her husband's taxes last year. It breaks my heart to think of them going to H & R Block. They might as well flush their money down the toilet.

To get back to when I found out she was blind.

It was before she introduced herself to me, because it was only after I knew she was blind that I offered to help her out. I wouldn't have said that to an ordinary woman, I'm not that considerate. I don't have *that much* free time on my hands. I tried volunteering once for one of those places that help people who are starting a small business. But I gave it up. I didn't care for the clientele. Too ignorant. Even though I spent my life with numbers, I was always aware of higher things. I tried to keep abreast of cultural goings-on. I used to love the theater, when there was anything worth seeing. I'll never forget *My Fair Lady.* Not like today, spending millions of dollars on a musical comedy about a Puerto Rican criminal. Some comedy.

I don't know when Ellie took her sunglasses off so that I knew that her eyes weren't right. Those eyes that weren't colorful. They reminded me of a seagull's eyes. Or pebbles, or some kind of rock. I hate to say that, because as I said Ellie is a good-looking woman. But it's better when she keeps her sunglasses on.

Of course I was a little nervous at first when she took her sunglasses off and I could see she was blind. Like I'd started out on the wrong foot. It did feel like that, like I'd missed a step and landed when I thought I had another step to go.

But I handled myself well. I said hello and that I saw she'd just moved in. Even though I was embarrassed about the word *saw.* I didn't let on. Just introduced myself.

* * *

It was only the second time we met that I noticed that sometimes she talked a little too loud. We met again at the elevator.

"It's Ronald, from upstairs," I said.

"Oh, hi, Ronald," she said. And it struck me as just a little bit too enthusiastic. And sometimes her smile is a little too wide. But I don't think she can help that. I did speak to her once about modulating her tone of voice. She thanked me for it. She said people were always afraid to criticize blind people's behavior, as if they were "emotionally weak." Those were the words she used, *emotionally weak.* I was impressed with that. I thought it was a good way of making the point. I probably should have told her that, but at the time I let it slip and I didn't think I should bring it up later. "In point of fact," she said, "most blind people are as tough as old boots." I liked that expression.

Our first encounter was because she needed help. She was having trouble getting her key to work in the door. It was a new lock, a little stiff the way they sometimes are. I worked on it a few times and it opened. But I told her that she shouldn't have to put up with that kind of thing. That she should ask the super to fix it.

"Which is a hopeless prospect, trying to get anything out of him," I said.

"Actually, Mr. Glevenko's been very kind to me," she said.

I didn't say anything. I figured, hope for the best. But in

my mind Glevenko's the scum of the earth. He's a Russian. A real *bullyock.* That's a Yiddish word that literally means bullock, but it's supposed to show a lack of refinement, to say the least. Strong back, weak mind. I don't care that Glevenko's Jewish. I've always known there's such a thing as Jews without refinement. I knew he was a Jew but he didn't seem Jewish to me. To me he was a Russian. A Cossack. On horseback in the shtetl, leading a pogrom. I couldn't help it. That was the way I saw him.

Glevenko thought he was a real ladies' man. When he went out on Saturday nights, he wore a black suede jacket, or maybe it was navy blue, I never got close enough to tell, and matching square-toed boots, also, of course, suede, which I implied by saying they were matching. He wore gold chains around his neck, and in the middle of his chest was some kind of iron cross like a Nazi. I guess it was to pick up non-Jewish women. Mind you he had a wife and children in Russia. He was supposed to be saving up money to bring them over. I'll believe that when I see it. Not that I ever will now.

He was catnip to women. You could hear, up and down the building. "Oh, Victor, when you have a minute," or "Oh, Victor, my faucet," or "Oh, Victor, my closet door needs to be fixed." Everybody knew he was fixing a lot of other things besides faucets and closet doors. Which is why half the women were batting their eyelids and saying, "Oh, Victor," this, and "Oh, Victor," that, and half of them were furious at him. And then there were the others—happily married women and men who weren't interested in him who were furious at him because he always took his own sweet time getting around to what you'd ask him to do. Although I have to say in all honesty, to say nothing of fairness, when he got around to things he was very good at them. He had a lot of mechanical ability. I think that's attractive to women. They like that he-man stuff.

Ellie's husband, George, wasn't much in the he-man line. You might have said it was because he was blind, but one of the things I learned from Ellie was that blind people weren't that different. You couldn't excuse or explain everything because of the blindness. "Blind people are like other people, only more so," she used to say.

Her husband was a big-shot engineer. I don't know what kind. Maybe chemical. I don't know how he did his work, with the blindness. He wasn't born blind, as I know I said before. I don't like to repeat myself. Repetition can get boring, which I have to watch out for. People hear you are, or in my case were, an accountant and they're ready to be bored before you open your mouth. One great thing about Ellie's and my friendship, we were always interesting to each other. Whatever I said, she was interested. And I learned a great deal from her. I only regret I didn't ask her more when I had the opportunity.

* * *

I don't think her husband talked to her much. He always seemed in a bad mood. Frustrated. I think things weren't going well at work. Or at least that's my explanation for his grumpiness. He was even grumpy with his dog. As Ellie told me, a blind person and his dog, or her dog, have what's called a symbiotic relationship. Ellie's relationship with her dog was excellent. "Hilda's my best friend," she said once, and as if she sensed I was a little hurt by that she said, "Well, one of them, anyway, and considering that we're in each other's company twenty-four hours a day, that's kind of a miracle." George and his dog, Ralph, didn't have a good relationship. Not like Ellie and Hilda. I thought that said something.

Ellie and I spent quite a bit of time in each other's company. Because of being just one flight up, and, of course, the blindness cut down on her mobility. I took to picking up groceries for her whenever I went to the store, and pretty soon we fell into the habit of morning coffee.

She gave me a key to the apartment. She said she liked thinking of me as one of the family. I told her that sometimes I liked to open the door and stand in the hallway just to listen to her playing the piano. Because that was what she did. She played the piano, professionally. She was a professional pianist. Although not professional exactly. She was a music teacher. She'd taught music in a school for the blind in Detroit. She hadn't been able to find work in New York. She was trying, but it's not easy. People have prejudices. Even though she was a very talented musician. I was grateful to her for reviving my interest in music, particularly the light classics.

I said I liked standing in the hall and listening to her, but I didn't want to disturb her, I just liked to hear her better. She said I didn't disturb her, although she could feel my presence on the back of her neck. She said that the hairs on the back of her neck stood up when someone entered her space. She said it was a kind of animal response of self-protection. Only, she said she never felt any need to protect herself from me. She said she always liked the sense of my presence in her space. She said I was her good angel. She said she could tell me anything and everything. She was wrong.

She shouldn't have told me about the feelings that *bullyock* Victor aroused in her. It's not the kind of thing a woman should tell a man, even if she's blind and he's on the elderly side. I wouldn't exactly say I was jealous. But the whole thing struck me as wrong. After all, she was a married woman.

That Victor liked listening to her music too. And sometimes he'd take his coffee break with her, and ask her to play the piano for him. But not classical. What he asked her to play was in my opinion crap. I asked why she gave in to his bad taste. That was when she told me more than I wanted to know. I guess it was my fault. But how could I have stopped her?

Because she said, in answer to my question, that she liked giving him pleasure. And if playing songs that were not exactly in her line gave him pleasure, that was what she wanted. He gave her things that she wanted, so she wanted to give him something back. She said that something about him, his presence, made her feel like a woman. Like an attractive woman, attractive to an attractive man. I noticed that she used the word *attractive* three times in one sentence, so I figured it was important to her. I asked her how she knew he was attractive. I took the chance of being rude. But she wasn't offended.

"You can just tell," she said. "Attractive people give off something, like animals. He gives off that musk."

Musk. I thought it was a disgusting word. Musk. Also I happened to know that the man was no good. Particularly in the department of the opposite sex.

Everyone knew what he did in the empty apartment. Fifteen-C, where the Lewisons used to live, that was vacant for months. Mrs. Grossman swears she saw him bringing a mattress up there. And we'd all see him going in there with a variety of ladies. Nobody said anything about it to the management, because, even if we didn't like his attitude, he was very mechanical. And we'd seen a lot worse, and we knew we could see much worse again. Everyone decided to turn a blind eye. That's another expression I would have used without thinking before I met Ellie, but I stopped for a while. Now there's no reason not to pick it up again.

I never told Ellie about the Lewisons' apartment. I

didn't want to shatter her innocence. Being blind had made her a very innocent person. Like a child. Like a beautiful child. I didn't want to have it on my conscience to spoil that. So I just let her go on with her "musk." I know she didn't know what she was talking about. I only wanted to protect her. I never wanted her to be hurt.

And that was why I did what I did. I couldn't stand seeing her hurt. When I saw the tears coming out of those poor sick eyes—it was strange, as if being blind, tears should have come from some other place on her body. But, of course, even if they couldn't see, they were eyes.

She told me everything that happened. She came up to my apartment, which she rarely did, just to cry.

"I'm a fool," she said. "I'm a goddamn fool."

I'd never heard her use bad language before either.

Supposedly he had this wife and child in Russia. But here he had God knows how many women but one in particular. A Spanish girl. Very brassy. He showed me a picture of her once, taken from the back. She was bent over, sticking her behind out, and she was looking at the camera over her shoulder. Thank God she had clothing on. As it was, I didn't know where to look.

Everyone in the building had seen him taking her to the Lewison apartment. Quite a lot. For a long time there was no one else going in there with him, only this Spanish girl. But nobody knew details. I could tell that sometimes he wanted to brag to me about her, but I didn't listen.

I guess what he did that upset Ellie wasn't his fault. Ellie had kept her feelings to herself, to be fair to him. So he asked her if she could do him a favor and I guess he had no way of knowing it would be hard for her. As I said, she'd never let on.

He told her that since his girlfriend was married they never got to appear in public together. So they never got to dance together, and his girlfriend particularly liked to dance. So he asked Ellie if she would play some of their favorite tunes on the piano so they could dance together in her living room.

Ellie was torn. She didn't feel she could say no. What reason would she give? She had no claim to him. There was nothing between them, except the way he made her feel when he called her "pretty girl," or "peaches and cream." I'd thought that myself, peaches and cream, who wouldn't think of that, the way she was complected, but I would never have said it. It would have seemed too familiar. But that wasn't the kind of thing Victor thought about.

She felt she had to do what he wanted, even though it broke her heart. She played the stupid songs they liked. "Feelings," and "Close to You." Real garbage. When she came to my apartment, it broke *my* heart. She said she ought to think of it as an interesting experience, because she'd never in her life been jealous before and jealousy was one of those basic human emotions that you shouldn't die without experiencing.

She just sat at my kitchen table and cried her heart out. "Oh, Ronald," she said. "You're such a comfort to me." Then she got up and left. With the dog, of course.

That should have made me happy, that she said I was a comfort to her, but it made me feel pathetic and old. It made me feel she thought about me the way she thought about her dog. *Comfort* was a word for someone who wasn't giving off musk.

So I suppose you'd have to say that what I did was spiteful. I called the landlord, anonymously, and I told him what was going on in the Lewison apartment, 15-C. He came, Johnny on the spot. He made Victor open the apartment. We could hear him shouting all over the building. He was a hothead.

Apparently Victor had a real little love nest up there. Candles, portable refrigerator, microwave. And the mattress that we all knew about. The landlord threw the microwave out the window. Everyone could hear the crash. Fifteen floors.

Victor had to pack his things up that day. He wasn't exactly given the time to say good-bye.

* * *

Ellie was very upset. I always thought she knew I had something to do with it, although she never said anything. But she had that kind of sixth sense about some things. She said that wasn't uncommon in blind people.

Things were never the same between us. I don't know why. Maybe I was giving off a new scent that she picked up, that made her uncomfortable. Maybe it was fear or shame. People don't like that, and she was very sensitive. Much more than most.

Pretty soon after Victor left, Ellie and her husband moved out. A loft in SoHo. They said they liked the sense of space. Most people would have said the light, but in their case that would have been irrelevant.

She gave me her address and told me to come by. But it's not a part of town I ever go to. Way down there. Why should I go into those old buildings that remind me of sweatshops? The kind of place my family wanted to get away from forever, worked and slaved so they wouldn't have to go near again. And people paying a fortune nowadays. Besides, I don't like those old elevators. I don't trust them. I worry about her with those elevators. I don't like to think about it.

* * *

And anyway, my friendship with Ellie wasn't that strong. It didn't have that much going for it. It was just that I got used to dropping by. It made sense because we were neighbors, and if we weren't neighbors, there wasn't that much to it. If we weren't neighbors, it didn't make any sense at all.

JASON BROWN

AFTERNOON OF THE *SASSANOA*

Jacob's father had business in the city that afternoon and the next morning. "Go with him," Jacob's mother said. "You two can spend the night and sign up for your preseason soccer the next morning. It will save me having to give you a ride down."

Jacob agreed to go, even though it took him away from the island and would involve a trip across to the mainland in the skiff and a seemingly endless hour's drive on the highway. Not bothering to bring a change of clothes, Jacob jumped off the back porch and followed his father down to the island's dock.

The fetch between Heron Island and the mainland darkened as Jacob's father, in the stern, thumbed tobacco into his pipe. After a few attempts he gave up trying to light the pipe in the wind, and as if this failure tumbled him toward another, he pushed away from the dock and started to row from the wrong direction, pushing the handles away from his chest. Jacob was in the oarsman's seat, and it was harder for his father, rowing this way, to keep the leathers from popping out of the locks. The bags under his father's eyes looked even heavier than usual, and a thin line of blood traced across his freshly shaved neck. His shoulders bunched as he reached forward, his already round face growing red and puffy after only a few strokes.

"You take it." His father pushed the oar handles toward Jacob. Even though it was not far to the dock on the mainland, they would blow downwind, toward Robinhood Cove, unless Jacob pulled as hard as he could. As a way of not looking at his father's face, he gazed through the Townsend Gut, the narrowest point between the island and the main, where the water funneled in and the wind whipped between the columns of tall pines, kicking up rows of chop.

"It's the best day for sailing we've had yet," his father said. Jacob shot a glance at the *Sassanoa* riding high on her white hull above the water, her nose pointing into the wind and jumping up like a Thoroughbred against her mooring tether.

"Let's go for a short sail, just once across the bay, and then I'll still have time to get to town."

"I thought you had to be there by four. We might not even make it if we start now."

"By five, five-thirty. I just have to meet the guy to have

him sign some papers and have someone rush them over to the courthouse before it closes."

Jacob didn't say anything. He had already said enough to his mother about not wanting to go to town. He wanted to sign up for soccer, but he hated anything that took him away from the island. Also, he and his father would be alone for the night, and then Jacob would have to hang around the house on Woodmont Street all day waiting for his father to finish work so they could drive back to the island.

He wondered if it was a good idea for his father not to leave enough time to get his client to sign the papers, and he knew that when his father rushed, he always drove too fast on the highway and sometimes got a ticket in the speed trap where Route One met the main highway. That would put him in a foul mood for the whole week. Jacob didn't want to say anything about not sailing, didn't want to screw up his chances of taking the boat out alone the next year, while his father was at work, when he could sail by himself down the coast to Five Islands. The tourists there, eating lobsters and clams, would look at him as though he had stepped into their lives from a past century. The year before, his father had said he could take the boat out when he was twelve, the same age Jacob's grandfather had let him go out alone, but this year his father changed his mind to thirteen. Jacob wasn't sure he would ever be old enough at this rate.

"We'll just go across the bay and back," his father said,

and nodded in the direction of the *Sassanoa.* Jacob pushed harder on the port oar and swung them around. The day was good for sailing. The pines swayed; the breeze southerly but cool. Jacob started to row for the island dock. His father's hand shot forward and wrapped around the starboard oar, shoving it into Jacob's chest so hard that it knocked the breath out of him.

"What about the boat bag?" Jacob asked.

"We're just going across the bay once."

His father looked away, apparently realizing he had accidentally been too rough. Jacob wasn't going to argue about the boat bag. Even his grandfather had gone without it on short sails—just to spite the yacht club guys and their overprecautions, he would say. Jacob's father opened his briefcase for the cell phone, unfolding the mouthpiece, and pushed power, bringing the clear buttons to life with yellow light. He dialed and held the phone to his head, reaching out with the other hand to grab the *Sassanoa.* Frustrated, he handed the phone to Jacob.

"When your mother picks up tell her we're just going across the bay and back before I head into town."

Jacob took the phone. His father rested his briefcase on the deck of the *Sassanoa,* balanced himself precariously on the middle seat of the skiff, and pulled himself up. Both Jacob and his mother hated having cell phones on the island, where they came to escape such things, and his mother was already upset about his father's rushing to the city three days into his vacation for an emergency meeting.

"You don't have your windbreaker," his mother said, after Jacob told her what they were doing.

"It's warm out."

"Tell her we're not going to be out long."

Jacob's mother heard her husband. "So call me from town tonight," she said. Jacob didn't know what to say. He said good-bye, his mother said good-bye, and he put the phone in the briefcase.

Jacob couldn't remember a time when they had not come to the island in the summer. Now that his grandmother was too old to stay on the island, Jacob came with just his mother and father. Jacob often helped his mother scrub the clothes against the washboard behind the cottage, using water they caught from the sky and stored in a large tank. Jacob's grandfather had been the pilot of Portland Harbor and his grandparents had lived on the island year round, without insulation and many of the other things the cabin still didn't have—things that Jacob wished their house in Portland didn't have either. Sometimes in the fall, after returning to Portland, Jacob refused to use the phone, lights, or running water, as a way of pretending he was still on the island.

As if they were trying to escape, or as if the rush that Jacob expected on the highway had already begun, his father tugged frantically at the sail ties, pulling out the boom crutch and tossing it carelessly under the foredeck, whereas Jacob had been taught to lash it forward to keep it from banging around once they were under way.

Things were done in a certain way on the island, not only because they had been done that way for sixty years but because it was the right way. Jacob had learned everything about the island from his grandfather. Now that his grandfather was gone, Jacob sometimes wondered if his father was forgetting things. The previous fall Jacob had had to remind him to spread wood chips beneath the *Sassanoa* in the boathouse, to absorb moisture through the winter. The fifty-year-old oak planks, cut from trees on the island, would get dry rot in one season without the wood chips, and he worried that his father did not think of it.

"Just tie the skiff up now," his father yelled. They had always tied the skiff to the stern until the *Sassanoa* was ready to sail. Otherwise the two boats would rub. Jacob moored the skiff to the buoy, as he had been told, and of course his father had not raised the main by then, so he had to sit on the deck and separate the two boats with his legs. His father tugged on the halyard, but it was stuck.

"Damn," his father grumbled. "Jacob, help me for a second." Jacob was reluctant to let the two boats alone, but his father was frustrated, so he pushed the dory off as far from the hull of the *Sassanoa* as he could and rushed back to hold the halyard while his father jiggled the runner free. The sail rose easily then, snapping at the air, and Jacob rushed back to the bow to find the rail of the skiff already rubbing against the *Sassanoa*'s white hull. He swore to himself, pushed the dory away, and leaned over the bow to see what damage had been done. He saw a scratch three inches long. It hadn't penetrated to the wood, but the skiff had gouged out several layers of white paint and left a green smudge. It would allow moisture closer to the wood. He should fix the scratch right away, as his grandfather had taught him to do, though the only way to take a scratch out was to haul the *Sassanoa* and repaint her entire hull. Jacob was trying not to think about it, but he knew they shouldn't sail now. Not with a scratch in the hull.

"Cast off," his father yelled. The sail was up, but the tiller was still lashed. Jacob untied the bowline but did not let go of the mooring buoy until his father freed the tiller. Then they drifted back with the wind until the sail scooped the air and leaned them to port. It was a perfect breeze. With the jib up they would move along nicely. The *Sassanoa* never moved very fast. She was nineteen feet on the waterline but otherwise very much like a Herreshof Bull's-eye, with a full keel and wide beam; Jacob's grandfather had designed her to transport his family and their supplies to and from shore.

Jacob raised the jib and tied down the sheet. His father held the tiller and the mainsheet, so Jacob had nothing to do except watch the skiff at the mooring become smaller as they tacked back and forth in the narrow space between the island and the mainland. As they came through the gut and faced the bay, the sails braced against the wind coming in off the ocean. His father loosened the main, leaned back, and eyed the telltales. The telltales had been his father's addition, after his grandfather's death, and Jacob knew they weren't right. He never looked at them when he sailed, but felt the boat's movement under him to find the wind. If the breeze was stiff but he felt no tension on the tiller and little heel, he was off the wind. His grandfather had taught him to rely as little as possible on sight. Eyes were no good in fog or darkness.

"I bet we can make Knubble Head in one tack," his father said. Jacob tried to gauge how the wind and tide would take them over the three quarters of a nautical mile. The wind was shifting around to the southwest, so they could head farther out, but then Jacob wondered how long it would take for them to get back. If the wind stayed southerly, or even if it moved completely westerly, they would have no problem on a broad reach plowing straight across the bay. Jacob looked around for the Coast Guard, but the bay was empty except for a few lobster boats and a trawler. They often sailed across the bay without the boat bag—the *Sassanoa* could handle any kind of rough weather that might come up unexpectedly. But the Coast Guard had fined them twice for not having life jackets; his father had tried to argue out of the ticket each time.

Jacob looked back at the granite face of Heron Island, jutting south like the prow of a ship. His mother was working beside the house on the island, taking the laundry in off the line. Inside the cabin the dead grandfather stared down with cold eyes at the dining room table from the framed photo on the wall. Jacob assumed it was the circumstances of the time that had made him hard. Jacob remembered when he had rowed over to the island with his grandfather in the winter to cut down a Christmas tree; the steam had risen from the water in white patches like ghosts and blown with the wind across the bay. The scene had seemed medieval; the cracked brown knuckles of his grandfather's hands moved toward him and away, rowing. Jacob removed his glove and dipped his hand in the water, which felt warm, like a bath, compared to the air.

Even now, Jacob thought, the year could have been 1878 on the island—nothing about the kerosene lamps or cast-iron pots suggested people elsewhere had ever seen electricity, and in the weeks they spent on the island each summer, depending on his father's work, Jacob forgot the appliances of their house in Portland, where his father rose and dressed in a suit each morning before driving off to a twelve-story glass building. From his office Jacob's father could see the bridge and the bay where his father had guided ships, and the ocean beyond, where his grandfather had fished the Grand Banks.

"Haul in the jib," his father snapped, and Jacob obeyed, even though he knew the jib would not come in any farther, not without spilling air and losing some of what his father wanted, which was to point higher so they could reach the Knubble in one tack, which got them nothing if they had to inch all the way there. His father pulled in the mainsheet, running the line down around the cleat. The *Sassanoa* heeled over in response. Rollers from a storm that had never reached shore pitched them up. Jacob did not worry. He and his grandfather had been out in fifty-knot winds. The ribs and planks creaked but nothing gave, not even the old hand-sewn sails. But she was weaker now since his grandfather's death.

As they approached the Knubble Lighthouse, Jacob saw tourists standing on the rocks raise their binoculars to examine them. The *Sassanoa* was an unusual sight, with its mahogany brightwork on deck, its white hull and red sails, the spars themselves varnished spruce cut from the forest on the mainland less than a mile from the island. Jacob saw a boy about his age borrow binoculars from his father and look out, and Jacob envied the boy for looking out at the boat, though he would rather be where he was, sailing her. It would be nice to have both. She sailed very nicely, not fast like these new fiberglass boats built with long fin keels and flat bottoms. Those were good for speed, but not for rollers and sudden winds. Jacob would take the *Sassanoa* in any bad weather over one of those ugly boats. The *Sassanoa* rolled over the swells and did not slap the spray back into the cockpit. A powerful, curling swell could punch a hole in the side of a glass hull, but the *Sassanoa,* with its thick oak planks, absorbed each blow like a prizefighter feeling for his opponent's strength.

"Let's sail over to Mauldin," his father said. "From there it'll be a straight shot back in."

Jacob looked down at his watch. "I don't know if you'll have time to make it into town if we don't head back now."

"It won't make much difference," his father called, looking up at the sail. "We can't miss a wind like this."

"I don't think we'll have enough time," Jacob said again, staring at the floorboards.

Instead of getting angry, as Jacob expected, his father smiled, looking up at the sail. "A wind like this will take us anywhere." Jacob looked at his father and saw his crooked yellow teeth and bumpy nose, the swell of fat girdling his jaw. For the first time he saw his father as he imagined a woman might see him, in the clear, unforgiving sunlight.

Jacob glanced up toward the southwestern sky, at a line of thick dark clouds moving toward them with the freshening winds. Already his father had to ease off on the mainsheet to accommodate the extra force. Thunderheads. "Head for shore when you see those," his grandfather said.

After a long tack they came up on the high granite side of Mauldin Island. The people in the house above sat on their porch looking in the direction of the thunderheads, probably discussing if they should secure the shutters. It was hard to predict what the weather would do, even when they could see it coming, but finally Jacob mentioned it.

"What about those thunderheads?"

"Those are thunderheads," his father said matter-of-factly. No smile this time. Suddenly, as a small cloud shaded the sun, his father looked down into the green water at the small ripples curling into the windward side of the hull. He seemed to be concentrating on a difficult decision.

The bow of the *Sassanoa* plowed through the water toward the rocks. The shallows dropped off immediately, but they were closing fast, fifteen yards, twelve, and still his father looked over the windward side. Jacob determined not to say anything and almost found himself hoping the boat would crash into the granite. He shook his head at the thought. Five yards away his father casually swung the tiller across and brought them about. Jacob unhitched the jib and cleated it on the starboard side. He readied himself to let the sail out for heading downwind, but his father kept them headed out of the bay, straight for New Wagon Harbor.

"I thought we were going to head in," Jacob said, trying not to sound anxious.

"I thought we would head out and sail through the 'trickiest bit of sailing in the East,' " his father said, quoting Jacob's grandfather. His father gave a quick nod in that direction they were heading, and Jacob saw the corner of his mouth rise as he leaned down to pull in the mainsheet.

"What about your client and signing those papers?"

"Fuck it. Just fuck it."

Jacob waited for him to say more, but his father studied the luff in the canvas where the main joined the mast. "Winds like this don't come around every day." He narrowed his eyes, pulling in on the sheet and carefully adjusting the tiller. Jacob had never seen him look so determined, not even when he worked. "We can make New Wagon Harbor in one tack."

He wondered about his father's work, if people would

be left waiting in town and if they would be angry at his father. Jacob had heard conversations over the last months between his mother and father about his father's practice, and Jacob was not sure everything was going well.

New Wagon Harbor, on the southern tip of the mainland, was formed by three small, burly islands nestled close into shore. They sailed within ten yards of the mainland on the port side, trying to edge into the harbor without tacking again. Jacob could see the pale, sharp rocks below the tidal line and the red keel that edged up toward the surface as they heeled over.

"How much room we got?" his father asked.

"You got it," Jacob answered.

"One tack."

They were inside the harbor, the mainland and dock to the left, the three islands to the right, and Jacob felt relieved. As if a hand had released its pressure on the mast, they tilted upright as the wind diminished behind the islands.

That wasn't the trickiest bit of sailing either. Now they were going to sail between the northern and eastern islands, where unmarked rocks spiked up from the bottom. Jacob thought the tide was too low, which was the only thing that made his grandfather describe this reef as tricky. They simply needed to know where the rocks were and to go at the right tide.

"Our momentum will carry us forward until we can

catch the wind again," his father said. "And I'll steer us around the rocks."

Jacob nodded, though he was doubtful. They couldn't see the rocks beneath the surface, but his father had sailed this many times before, with his own father and alone. Jacob didn't know how shallow it would be. The rollers crashed into the windward side of the islands, but the water in the harbor was calm.

"Pull the jib in," his father said. The wind would come around and they would heel, so they would draw less. That would help.

Jacob uncleated the jib and recleated it, but there was no point—the jib had been lashed too tightly to begin with.

"Good." His father pulled in on the mainsheet, preparing for the wind. The tide was moving out, lowering every minute now. Several families were eating lunch on the pier outside the Lobster Shack. They stopped cracking their lobsters for a moment to stare at the red sails of the *Sassanoa,* gliding by from sheer momentum on the flat water. One of the younger kids sitting on the bench leapt up when she saw the sails and raced toward the end of the pier. Her mother ran after, yelling the girl's name. The girl could have run off the end of the pier. She stopped at the last minute, though, and pointed at the red sails.

Jacob could see twelve, ten yards ahead, the line of blue water marking the wind. As they grew closer, the wind receded and the shallow rocks appeared, yellow and white beneath the surface. Jacob watched the blue patch of wind on the water draw back like a snake into its hole and vanish. Now they were drifting straight onto the rocks, with no wind coming around the island to make them heel. His father knew and only had a few seconds to decide what they would do. He could steer them gradually to the left, but with no wind there was little point in throwing the tiller over. They would still drift forward. Before either could act or speak Jacob saw just behind his father's head a patch of dark blue water, a stiff gust, advancing from the north. Jacob barely had time to release the jib, though he realized later that it was the wrong thing to do. The wind caught inside the loose jib and lurched them straight forward at no heel. His father lowered his jaw and put his hands out to the side, as if some enormous creature had lifted him off the ground and was preparing to swallow him whole. Jacob waited for the sound, but halfway through the passage none came and he thought maybe they would make it all the way through. Then came the thud that seemed distant, lurching the *Sassanoa*'s bow down and her stern into the air. The wind caught the trimmed mainsail and pulled them sideways off the rock. When broadside to the wind and going over, Jacob finally unleashed the mainsail and let the boom fly. The wind spilled out; they were off the rock. His father leaned over the side of the boat to check for damage.

"No harm done," he said and grabbed the tiller. There had only been a thud, Jacob thought. His father took the helm back and steered them toward the channel. Jacob trimmed the jib, and they sped along with the wind and rocks behind them. The collision seemed never to have happened, and Jacob knew they would not talk about it—as if it were a secret they would have to keep from his dead grandfather.

Outside the harbor the wind blew twice as strong, and the swells rose high into the air. The hull planed. Jacob sat on the rail and adjusted the jib sheet, while his father sat on the transom so he could see over the bow. When they rose to the top of a swell, they could see out to sea as if from the top of a mountain. The bow sliced up one side of the wave and the stern coasted down the other side, just as his grandfather had designed her to do, and Jacob was immensely proud in that moment, thinking of his grandfather's mind and hands creating such an efficient and worthy craft. More than that: the *Sassanoa* was a work of art, perfectly balanced between the wind and the ocean, that sat at her mooring in the morning calm as a sleeping dove.

Jacob looked back at his father, who grinned like a child, his open mouth and bright wide eyes pointed up at the red sails as if the very idea of the wind moving a boat over water at such a speed was a discovery he had just made for the world.

As they coasted down a swell, Jacob leaned over and placed his hand on the side of the hull. He did not think of turning around even as they passed Damirscove Island. He could see in the windows of the old Coast Guard station there; at a certain height he could see in one window and out another. Europeans had settled on the treeless island, he knew, before Plymouth or Jamestown. They had fished there, and lived in cold shacks. Several hundred years later the Coast Guard had come, and now they were gone too, and the island was empty except for the terns, gulls, herons, and snowy egrets who swarmed over the grass.

After Damirscove there were no other landmarks to gauge distance over water, and Jacob did not look back except to check his father's eyes darting from the sails to the ocean in perfect concentration. Jacob didn't care how far they sailed, as long as his father continued to smile.

Jacob looked up at the sail and noticed how the pressure of the wind moved from one side to the other as his father shifted the lines and tiller. Some of the wind spilled out the side of the sail, swirled around back, and caused a luff. With a slight adjustment they were back on track. Then Jacob noticed a frayed stay. Three or four of the metal threads that twisted around each other had snapped, which left two or three at the most to hold all the weight of the sail and the wind. Any number of bad things would happen, Jacob thought, if the rear stay broke. The mast would snap immediately, and might drag the boat over with this strong a wind. The weight of the keel would probably keep them upright. Even so, without the sail there was only the paddle. No motor. Jacob promised himself he would check all the rigging the next day.

"Dad, look." Jacob pointed up at the stay and as he pointed he knew he was also pointing a finger at his father for not keeping the boat up to his grandfather's standards.

His father glanced up and saw the fray but did not seem concerned.

"It'll hold."

The wind did not vanish immediately, as often happened, but gradually, to Jacob's relief, until it was no longer necessary for his father to concentrate so hard on their heading. Jacob could tell his father's mind was on some other worry, probably something to do with work.

"We should head in," Jacob said. He hadn't even looked back for some time. He wanted his father to be the first one.

His father did look and raised his eyebrows, not in shock but surprise, so Jacob looked back too. They were a good distance from shore. The wind usually switched in the evening, after a lull. This was that lull. They would just have to wait for the switch. With any luck it would be a south or west wind. In any case, the water around the *Sassanoa,* for as far as they could see in all directions, was smooth and dull gray-green.

Jacob never noticed the cold when the sails were full, when there was action, but now, in the stillness, he rubbed the goose bumps on his arms.

His father pulled his sport coat collar up around his neck and looked down at the bilge. "Damn!" he yelled, and yanked his briefcase off the floor. He brushed the water off the leather surface. "I don't think any water got inside." At first Jacob thought he was talking about the *Sassanoa.*

The sails were swaying now, like curtains, in the dim light. The horizon had just turned orange. The night was going to be clear, though fog might even roll in from offshore. For the first time Jacob noticed that his sneakers were soaked. That's why he was so cold. Under way, he seemed to lose all sensation, but now he could see that his feet rested in water that had hidden in the bilge while the boat heeled. Their bow had dipped, riding the swells, but Jacob hadn't seen any water coming over.

His father let go of the tiller and the mainsheet. With no wind they couldn't control the *Sassanoa*'s direction. Jacob looked at the back of his father's hands, resting on top of the briefcase. With the dried sea salt on the tanned skin, Jacob thought his father looked like a man who had been out to sea a very long time, though the briefcase and suit jacket made it seem as if he was just on the way to the office. Jacob understood that the *Sassanoa* was leaking through the bilge, probably where the keel was bolted to the hull. When they thudded against the rock in New Wagon Harbor, they must have loosened the joint.

"I think we're taking on," Jacob said.

"I know," his father said without looking up. "I'm thinking."

Jacob was silent. He decided he had better think too. As a matter of pride his grandfather had never kept a motor on board. The hand pump bailer was on the island, with the life jackets and flares, in the boat bag. His father went under the deck and rummaged around. He came out a moment later holding the anchor, a twenty-pound aluminum hook attached to a length of chain and rope. The water had risen two inches above the floorboards and was still rising. Jacob wondered how far they were from shore—maybe a mile, maybe more. More. A lobster boat motored by on its way home a little ways to the west, but neither Jacob nor his father thought to wave. The boat would not have seen them anyway.

His father held the paddle in one hand and the anchor in the other. Suddenly he stood up on the deck and waved the paddle in the direction of the lobster boat. "Hey, hey." They could see the man in yellow waders behind the wheel, looking forward, not back.

Jacob had never in his life seen his father or grandfather call for help while on the water. His heart pounded, and he was no longer cold or tired. He had been thinking about his mother's shepherd's pie, but now he saw what he should have seen before.

"What are we going to do?"

His father sat down. "We'll be fine. Let's see what the problem is down there." He lifted the hatch in the floorboards and stared down through the water to the bottom of the bilge. The compartment narrowed to the shape of a V, where Jacob could see the keel bolts protruding. His father removed his jacket, folded it carefully on top of his briefcase, and reached his hand down into the bilge.

"I can feel the water flowing in around one of the bolts.

I think." He lifted his arm out. All the rollers had vanished now and the water was flat for as far as they could see. His father removed his shirt. Jacob was startled by the white skin and curled black hairs. He recognized the future shape of his own body, but had trouble imagining himself covered with that much hair. His father ripped the shirt on a cleat, tore it into strips, and leaned back into the bilge. The water was deep enough now that he had to crane his neck and left arm up to keep his face from going underwater. He gave up trying and plunged both his arms and his head under the water. Jacob watched numbly as his father's back muscles bulged and strained against the skin. He popped out a moment later, dripping and gulping for air.

"I wrapped the cloth around the bolt. Hand me the anchor and I'll pound it down. That should wedge the cloth in and stop the leak."

Jacob handed the anchor to his father, who went back down underwater. Jacob heard the thud of the metal anchor smashing against the top of the bolt and occasionally the sound of his father missing and hitting the wooden spine. His father came up for air and went back down. Finally he rested back and set the anchor down. "That should do it."

Jacob nodded. His father was shivering violently. "Put on your jacket, Dad."

"Yeah." After wrapping himself in the jacket for a moment and rubbing his arms, his father looked intently at Jacob. "We shouldn't have tried the trickiest bit."

"We'll fix it when we get back. We should probably replace those bolts anyway."

"You're right about that. Those bolts must be twenty-five years old. This is an old boat, you know. Let's get this water out of here. You start, will you. You'll have to use what's left of my shirt to sop it up, and then I'll start paddling."

Jacob picked up the shirt and soaked it in the water but quickly realized his father was not thinking right. Instead of using the shirt, Jacob took off his shoe and started to scoop out the water. "The tide's going out," he said.

"I know."

They were moving farther away from shore. His father paddled as Jacob scooped up water and dumped it over the side. His father kept looking down at his son, and Jacob guessed what he was thinking. He wanted to somehow hide it from his father, he didn't want his father to get angry at himself, but Jacob couldn't help it—the water was still rising.

His father sat down and stared back into the bilge. His feet were wet and he was shivering again. Jacob looked down, too, but couldn't see the bottom. His father removed his jacket again and thrust himself beneath the water. He stayed down so long Jacob almost touched the white skin of his father's back to make sure he was all right. Then his father burst out and stumbled back across the boat, landing against the tiller.

"Damn. It's not the bolt. There's a crack in one of the lower planks. One of the ribs must have pushed out when we hit and split the planks or something. I don't know, I can't patch it from inside."

His father's eyes widened when he saw his briefcase sitting on one of the seats. He lunged across the boat and fumbled with the latches.

"Let me," Jacob said, rising and standing next to his father, but his father pushed him away.

"I got it." The two latches clicked up and the briefcase popped open. His father grabbed the phone with his numb hands. He had to cradle it in one palm and aim with the index finger of the opposite hand at the power button. Jacob could see his father's teeth gleaming in the moonlight, but he turned his attention to the phone and waited for the yellow lights to appear on the panel. Nothing happened. His father pushed again, and again.

"The battery's dead. Didn't you turn the power off?" His father looked at the phone in total disbelief, and then at Jacob, who, to avoid his father's eyes, also looked at the phone. He tried to remember if he had pushed the power button after talking to his mother. His father let out an awful noise, half growl, half scream, and threw the phone toward shore. Jacob heard it plop like a small stone. His father picked up his briefcase, too, swung it against the deck of the boat with a crack, and then hurled that out as well. The white papers fluttered through the air like a flock of panicked terns before drifting slowly to the water and vanishing. The open briefcase tipped sideways and sank from view.

His father watched the place where it had been. Jacob watched his father and thought that they could have used the briefcase to bail. Maybe they could stay ahead of the leak until morning, when someone would see them for sure. "Maybe someone will see us out here tonight," he said.

His father looked up at the rigging, his shoulder blades pinching together. "Not with red canvas. We'll have to patch the crack from the outside. Hand me my shirt there and the anchor."

Jacob rested them on the deck as his father removed his shoes and slacks, groaning when his body slid into the cold water. The white arm came up and grasped the shirt and anchor. Then he put the anchor back on the deck.

"You'll have to dangle the anchor over the side for me while I use the edge of it to stuff the rag into the crack." His father's voice was already shaky, and his teeth chattered.

Jacob leaned over the side and watched his father vanish into the dark water.

"Give me a little more slack," his father said after coming up for air. Then he went back down again, and Jacob heard faint taps on the hull. His father came back up for air. "It's a long, narrow crack," he said. "It must bend inward but we can't get to it from the inside without ripping up the floor. Even then I think it's out of reach from the inside."

Jacob didn't want to say anything. He wasn't sure of the situation. His father went down again, tapped, and came up. This time he let out a long moan before sucking in air and going back down. Tapping turned to banging. Jacob could see the outline of the silver anchor swinging through the water below. His father was swinging as hard as he could through the water at the crack. Jacob had an idea which plank it was. The last thud was muffled. He looked down to see his father pulling back on the anchor.

"No!" Jacob said, but it was too late. His father pulled the anchor out and then came up for air. Jacob pulled the anchor aboard and reached his own arm down into the bilge. He could not reach the plank his father had been hitting, but now he could feel the flow of water rushing in where the anchor had made a gash.

"I'm too cold," his father said.

Jacob turned and wrapped his hands around one of his father's arms and pulled. His father kicked and lunged up, eventually getting his stomach over the gunwale and grabbing the edge of the seat. Jacob put his hands and arm around his father's waist, feeling the hair on his father's back press against his face, and tugged. The flesh was cold to his lips and hands, and Jacob was afraid to let go, even when his father was safely on the seat.

His father pulled away, rose to his feet, and found the anchor. He dropped it, and then clamped it between his hands and swung it over his head like an ax. The anchor bounced off the deck and fell to the floor. His father reached into the water and lifted it over his head again.

"No, no!" Jacob reached for his father, but the man was using the last of his full strength to swing the anchor against the deck. This time the anchor bounced into the ocean. They both watched as the chain and fifty feet of rope snaked out of the boat, snapped into the air, and disappeared. Jacob felt embarrassed for having cried out.

His father sat down on the seat. The water rose almost to his knee. Jacob shook, but his father was beyond that stage. His eyes drooped.

"We'll have to swim." His father barely mumbled, he was so groggy with cold.

Jacob nodded, but knew that was impossible. The tide had taken them farther out. Even in late August the water was cold, and they wouldn't have much time before hypothermia set in. Jacob was an excellent swimmer. He swam for a team at school, but that was in eighty-degree water at an indoor pool. The distance to shore would take him an hour and a half. A long string of lights followed the shoreline of New Wagon Harbor and seemed close enough to touch.

"You swim for shore and get help."

Jacob couldn't see his father's lips moving. "No."

"Don't argue. Take the paddle and swim as well as you can. Don't let go of it. Go now."

Jacob stood on the gunwale with the paddle in his hand, looking down into the water. The deck was less than a foot off the surface now. He eased himself in with the paddle gripped in his hand.

"I'll be right back," Jacob yelled, but there was no response. He could see the silhouette of his father's head and thought about checking on him, but decided he had better keep going, focusing on the brightest light on shore, probably someone's dock, and kicking with all his force. He felt strong at first, but then grew stiff, his limbs moving in slow motion. He looked behind him. The outline of the sails seemed lower in the water. He turned and kicked harder, afraid to lose sight of the dock but also thinking maybe the wind would still come up. Soon he could barely move his legs, and the water felt warmer as he turned onto his back to rest. His thoughts slowed. Tomorrow, he thought, they would tow the *Sassanoa* to the island and patch the hole. But the dark triangle set against the stars sank into the blue-black horizon, and there was no sign of the pale shoulders and arms of the man who had promised him all those summer afternoons when he would finally sail alone.

FREDERICK BUSCH

DEBRIEFING

I knew the man in the elegant gray-black suit who sat in the Windsor chair next to mine because he had recruited me, and I had brayed about him and about my service to the security of all the Western world to Dr. Ann Paulus while we betrayed her husband and attended seminars about—what else?—the heart. Lipsted, my recruiter, moved his chair so that he sat at an angle to me, I suppose to see my reactions to the questions of his colleague, who sat behind the desk. The colleague, Dennis Schultz, wore a brown sport coat in Donegal tweed over a tan V-neck sweater, and he consulted, and typed into, a laptop computer. He used his right hand, and his left seemed to me to lie in his lap, although the computer's screen partly blocked my view.

"I know you as Morton Green," Lipsted said.

I said, "That's who I am."

"First rate," he said. "Now, you broke your glasses in Ireland, I think. You stayed in the Great Western."

"Best Western," Schultz said.

"Great Southern," I told them.

Lipsted raised his eyebrows and nodded. Schultz typed.

"At the airport," Schultz said, looking up.

"They say *on* the airport for some reason," I said.

Lipsted said, "I ought to remind you, I guess, that you agreed to make the courtesy call, and you agreed to be debriefed."

"That's this," I said. "The debriefing, right? Here I am."

"We're grateful for your cooperation," he said, "assuming we can get it."

I said, "I stayed at the Great Southern Hotel, which is on Shannon Airport." I was looking at Lipsted's shoes, which were black and glossy. I wore wide lightweight walking shoes because of the gout, and I wondered if they seemed shabby by comparison. "Oh. And I did break my glasses, yes."

As if I'd praised him, Schultz looked up from the keyboard and smiled a tight, victorious smile. He looked as if he might shave every other day. And his Windsor knot was as large as a young child's fist.

"You arrived on the morning of the ninth?"

I nodded.

"Took a cab to the hotel, I assume."

"Walked," I said. "The hotel is, you know, right on the airport."

"I for one will never forget," Schultz said. Lipsted grinned pretty mirthlessly.

"Then I slept," I said.

"No breakfast?" Lipsted asked. "Nothing else? Shower? Phone call? Talk show on the telly? They do have those, don't they?"

"They have everything we do," Schultz said. "Mr. Green, why wouldn't you have safety glass in them?"

"In my glasses?"

He nodded.

"I guess I should get that. I wear the tinted glass."

"It gets darker in bright light," Lipsted said.

"So they really did break," Schultz said.

"The wing came off the frame."

Schulz said, "Ah. So the *lenses* didn't break. Was it the screw, that little brass screw that goes into the hinge?"

"Right on the money," I said.

"So for that, the screw that holds the wing, you took a cab into—where?"

"The bell captain suggested an optometrist. I took a cab into Ennis, the town's called."

Schultz nodded.

Lipsted asked, "Are you tired? Have we gone on too long? Would you like a break?"

"No," I said, "I just never did one of these before. I'm not sure, in fact, what it is we're actually doing."

"A routine debriefing of a collateral asset," Schultz said.

"Me."

"You."

Lipsted said, "We do this with any number of businessmen and -women, literary people, teachers, students, a broad cross-section of Americans who seem to enjoy helping their country."

"They *are* the country," I decided that I had to say.

"A lot of people would consider using a paper clip," Lipsted said. "You straighten one and stick it through the hinge and then you break it off or fold it around the wing. You've probably done that at one time or another."

"I probably have."

"So why, do you think, did you this time *not* do it? And go to the trouble and expense of taking a cab wherever. That's a pain in the ass, if you're jet lagged and looking for someone to fix your eyeglasses."

"No," I said, "I didn't do it when I was jet lagged. I did it later in the afternoon, after I slept. And the bell captain gave me an address. Why are we talking about this?"

"Contextualization," Schultz said, typing.

"Humor us," Lipsted said, recrossing his legs and pulling at his trouser pleats. "It's the way we work. Get it all pinned down, then we can understand the entire arc of action as a gestalt. All right? So. We have you sleeping, bell captain, taxi, optometrist. What was the street?"

"No idea," I said.

"Make any phone calls?" Schultz asked. He squinted, as if his eyes were exhausted or as if he'd recently started wearing contact lenses. In a photo on the wall, Schultz shaking hands with the Vice President, he wore wire-framed glasses.

"Besides the bell captain," Lipsted said.

"I called the optometrist's, to make sure they'd be open."

"Number obtained from the bellman," Lipsted added.

"Bell *captain,*" Schultz said.

"I guess concierge, you'd say," I said.

As is so often true with the concierge, he seemed to know about us and not at all to care. He probably knew right away, though I'm sure he heard from the waitress who came to my room with our orders. Long service in the lobbies of hotels, especially a lobby as small as that of the Shannon Great Southern, no doubt trains a man to spot the tall, pale, nervous American leaning over, as if trying to enfold, the small, athletic, nervously alert woman who arrives with the passengers of his planc but who pretends loudly, as he does, that they have, that moment, unexpectedly met. Since they are Americans, they travel in children's clothes—each is wearing soft white sneakers, floppy jeans, shirts hanging out at the waist—and each is certain that the staff of what looks like a long, low, stucco motel will have lost their reservations and canceled their rooms. On the stairs to the second floor, as I hefted her bag as well as my own—"Here!" I bellowed. "Let me give you a hand, Dr. Paulus!"—I hissed, as we reached the doors, "I'm doing a little job for the Department of State."

Lipsted knew of me through friends, Turkish dissidents

at Georgetown, one of whom was an author of mine, and he approached me through them so that I'd feel ashamed of saying no. I was, so I said yes, and I agreed to what Lipsted had called an innocent small run. Hence the braying to Ann, whom I was desperate to impress with a coin of some new denomination. For she knew me, she had known me, and she was determined to give me up. Like a boy who walked on his hands, or who hit a home run, or who chattered loudly of once having done so, I told her about the Department of State between my bouts of nagging.

She lay on her stomach, her face in the pillow, and she submitted to my tracing her vertebrae until I reached the cleft of her buttocks. There, I delicately made the feathery tracks of what I saw, behind my closed eyes, as topographical delineations of her flesh. And then, shifting outside of my interior dark, I traced trails down the back of each thigh. And, instead of permitting our silence to *speak,* or to save us from speaking, I had, apparently, to tell her, "If your marriage was a huge mistake, this will count as the hugest. We're all that we *have.*" I could hear my presumptiveness dying into a whine, and knew that I deserved what I was bound to hear.

"Morty," she said, half into the pillow, and therefore as if she were far away, and therefore hurting me—permitting me to tell myself that I was hurt—because she was somehow distant, "my marriage was a mistake. Most people's marriage is a mistake. Marriage is where you go to *make* your mistakes. I am raising my children pretty well. I tend to not kill my patients. I am awkward in bed, but not all that bad, I'm told."

"Not by me. *I* tell you you're wonderful. Who tells you different?"

"Thank you."

"No, who do you go to bed with?"

"Morty, stop."

"Ann: who?"

"Charles is who, for godsakes."

"I thought we agreed you'd cut that out."

"Idiot."

"There's no law a woman has to go to bed with her husband. So many women don't. The majority of women in English-speaking countries don't. Women in Francophone countries don't. So don't. All right?"

She said, "Fine. I won't."

"How'll I know you aren't anymore?"

"You won't, Morty. And you know why."

"You don't just stop seeing a man if you love him."

"Another Morton Green law of nature," she muttered into the pillow.

"No," I said, "now you have to say you love me. Then I get to badger you about leaving your husband."

"So you can help me raise my kids."

"I'd be all right."

"You'd be terrible. You're selfish, neurotic, and altogether too cute."

"I am cute, aren't I?"

She turned over, and I began to map the rest of her.

Lipsted poured coffee from a white plastic carafe into a cup decorated with the State Department seal. He spilled some into the saucer, and when he tried to wipe the coffee with his thumb, I saw his hand tremble.

"That's fine," I said.

"I can *clean* a little coffee up," he said between his teeth. He used the stiff, luxuriant-looking handkerchief on the saucer, then he wiped his hands dry, then refolded it into his suit-coat pocket. "Like new," he said.

Though I didn't know what he was referring to, I smiled, and Schultz smiled, as if to signal his approval of my cooperation.

"The conference," Shultz began.

"Medico-legal something or other of cardiac bypass procedures," Lipsted said.

"We publish medical texts," I said.

"Textbooks," Schultz said as he typed. Then: "We know this."

"The conference," Lipsted asked, "it was held on the hotel."

"Yes," I said. "At the hotel."

"You're not yanking us around," Schultz said.

"That's correct," I answered. "Why would I do that? How would it work, what would happen, if I got up and left? This isn't a great deal of fun."

"Serving your country can be hard work," Schultz intoned.

"You were kidding," Lipsted said. "Am I right? Because

no responsible adult citizen would agree to setting up this kind of a deal and then decide to blindside the government of the United States out of *pique.*"

"What was the name of the woman, Mr. Green?" Schultz was resting his chin in his typing hand, his elbow on the desk. He said, "We have her as Powlus."

"Paulus," I said. "And I'd say pissed off, not pique. You two are a matched set of bullies."

"Not matched," Schultz said. With his right hand he picked up the sleeve of his left arm and brought it into sight. The hand was shrunken, curled inward at a severe angle, and it looked blue-white. The nails somehow made me think of teeth. "Mr. Lipsted here has two sound hands. I have one. That makes us an unmatched set. Not to mention *his* wife irons his underwear. I acquired this asymmetry in Jerusalem. Car bomb. You read about it. You just didn't know I was there. Just as we didn't know the PLO or the Pan-Arab Jihad, or the Brotherhood of the Martyred Palestinian Children—nobody ever took credit—was there parking the laundry van outside the rare book dealer I used as a drop. I mean, we don't know if it might have been the *Jews,* who can get very freaky about West Bank settlements or the Wall or population purity or anything else. All this is about knowing. Consider this the Office of One-handed Epistemology. And do cut the shit."

I said, "Dr. Ann Paulus, P-A-U-L-U-S. She's a surgeon."

"Thank you," Lipsted said. I heard the saucer rattle at the cup.

"Here it is," I said. "I flew to Shannon from Kennedy on the six-something at night. I got in at dawn. I slept. I guess I flailed around and broke my glasses. I got them fixed in the city. I came back and ate and slept, and the next day I went to the meeting, in the same hotel, on shunts. I was after one of the speakers, a Dr. V. Ramaranda, to do a section on shunts for a revised edition of our cardiac procedures book. I had agreed to have a drink with a man from Turkey if he invited me. He did. I did. He loaned me his pen when I made a note on a napkin. I'd been told he might. After he did, I shook his hand and went up and went to sleep and left for home before lunch."

"And the pen?"

I took it out of my pocket and placed it on Schultz's desk. It was a cheap white plastic pen with a green plastic cap. On its side the pen said *Great Southern.* Schultz stared at it fondly.

Lipsted asked, "What did the gentleman say?"

"That he'd do the article."

"Holy shit," Schultz said.

"I'm sorry. It's my little spy joke. I apologize. The other gentleman talked about the rise of fundamentalism in the academic and governmental spheres, and he said he was grateful for the military adopting a hard line toward the Muslim extremists. He called it an 'infection.' "

Lipsted said, "He used that word."

"Yes."

"It's the kind of word," Lipsted said, "you might expect to hear at such a conference."

"Of course," I said. "It means something in code?"

"Debriefing," Lipsted said, as if apologizing, "tends to go one way. We ask, you answer."

It reminded me of Ann, complaining that I demanded much and told, finally, little. "Morty Green, the sex spy," she'd whispered, when we were sore, tired, and happier than miserable for a couple of minutes. "What if I made demands? Would we be better off?"

"I'll do anything you say."

"Never," she said. "You're impervious to *say*. I'd have to coerce you."

"Would you consider coercing me?"

I felt her shake her head. "I will only consider our stopping. No more talking about it. I'm taking a later plane so I can stay here and understand how terrible I feel, and then we're not doing it anymore, anyplace else, no more conferences, no more planned chance meetings ever again. Nobody ever said you're not supposed to feel lousy in your life. I think that's a problem with us. We thought we were entitled to feel good. We were acting like patients. From now on, we have to think like doctors."

"That's why I dropped out of med school."

"Flunked out," she said.

"Why are you kissing me? Why are you—"

"Because I *love* you, stupid."

"Right," I said. "That's right. So leave Charles and let's get, you know, together."

"Did you say married?"

"I might have."

"We can't."

"But *why*?"

"Because I'm leaving you, Morty. I told you that."

"I give up."

"You never give up."

"You're *counting* on me giving up."

I had swept my arm out, and I knocked the water carafe, the clock radio, and my glasses off the bedside table and against the wall. I heard everything hit.

She put her hand on my throat and gently pressed. I lay back, and she squeezed.

"Ann," I said.

"I feel your voice," she said. "It's pushing up into my hand. I'm holding what you say on my skin. And your pulse: you're a strong, healthy man, Morty. The prognosis is you'll live."

"Sir?"

I suppose I blinked at Lipsted.

He asked, "Are you all right?"

I said, "That's all that I remember."

Lipsted asked, "Did our friend say anything about medical practices?"

"No."

"Social life? Concerts? Art exhibitions?"

"He mentioned rugs," I said. "He called them carpets. He suggested I might want to have him send some kilims to me at home. I said sure. You know, in case it was a password or something about transmitting documents."

Schultz said to Lipsted, "Anything?"

Lipsted shook his head.

"No," Schultz said, "I can tell you we had no paroles established on a carpet theme."

"I'd say you've bought yourself a couple of rugs," Lipsted said. "Give them to your wife as a gift."

"We aren't married anymore," I said.

"Ouch," he said, looking at Schultz.

"We thought there was a trial separation," Schultz said.

"Once upon a time. Then the trial was over."

"Guilty," Schultz said.

I asked, "Of what?"

He smiled as if we were friends.

Lipsted asked, "And Dr. Paulus?"

"Is *she* a government person?" I asked. "Does she do what I did?"

"I can tell you she isn't an asset," Lipsted said. "I can tell you that much. She isn't one of ours. Never employed, never used. You and Dr. Paulus are your own, shall we say, affair. While the other stuff is ours."

Schultz picked up the pen and put it down. "Your government is grateful," he said.

"Couldn't he just have mailed you the pen? Or the information that's in it?"

Lipsted set a file folder on the carpet beside his chair. He said, "No."

"Never," Schultz said. "Epistemology doesn't go through the mails."

Lipsted said, "You don't mail explosives, and you don't mail an international culling. Nor studies of the acquisition thereof. It's a federal law."

"Of nature," she had said. "Laws of nature governing the behavior of men and women in hotels in the Republic of Ireland include the urge to acquire sweets, and that the woman wear the man's striped business shirt so she looks cuddly and innocent and nevertheless piece of ass-y, and that the man reclaim it one slow little button at a time."

"Room service won't deliver this late," I had said. "I'll go downstairs, though, and out to the terminal. I'll bring you something. I'll be back in a little while."

To what I thought of then as her own surprise, she said, and really seemed to mean, "Morty, thank you. Thank you. This is right."

And, to my own astonishment, I went. I watched her lie in bed beneath the duvet while I put on jeans and shoes, no socks, and a dark T-shirt. I didn't kiss her, and I didn't try to preserve the sight of her, wearing my shirt in my bed. I went downstairs and out, across the parking lot and over lawns, under a bright moon and a high gray sky. I heard the harsh coughing of rooks from the flat roof of the hotel. I went through the rows of parked rental cars, lit by green-gray lights on high metal stanchions, and into the arrivals terminal. It wasn't lighted, but was made not dark, with an exhausted-seeming fluorescence. It was a building that took its meaning from what people did inside it, and now it was empty except for a couple of unspeaking women in dark green coveralls who slid wide brooms across the floor. A haggard-looking man in a rumpled shirt and undone necktie stared at me from under his brows while he made a calculater rasp and clack under one bright lamp at an auto rental counter. The concessions were closed behind corrugated metal shutters, and in the thin light, the women pushed their brooms, which made rasping noises on the dark linoleum floor. Papers rattled, and something fell, and I fed coins into brightly lighted machines until I had an armful of sodas and candy bars and crisps.

Now, I saw, men and women in uniform walked silently from the doors at the far end of Arrivals and through a couple of swinging doors. It was a little before four in the morning. Flights would be here in a couple of hours. I waited to see whether the concession stands would open, or if someone might deliver early newspapers. One of the cleaning women had stopped working and seemed to be studying me.

I lifted my chin as if to challenge her, but she simply stood a moment more and then went back to pushing her broom, and I left Arrivals, carrying the sweets most adults will buy only for watching films or traveling long distances. As I had a day or so before, I went among the cars, and over flower beds and lawns, toward the Great Southern Hotel. Yellow had poured across the dull gray of the sky, and it seemed to have dropped lower. I had to kick on the door until the night man came, and then I had to ask him if he would hold the sweating cans and crackling packets while I found my key to prove I was a guest. He wore a white shirt and a necktie and a metal pin that said Ethan. He wore striped uniform trousers, and old-fashioned carpet slippers over his socks. His hair seemed combed, but his long, pale face looked rumpled, and I apologized for disturbing him.

"I don't mind at all, sir. It's an aspect of my job, isn't it? Though we'd have had the chars in soon enough on their shift, mind you, and the doors unlocked," he said. "You'd have managed to get in with your snack."

"I was in a little bit of a hurry, I suppose."

"Well, you're American, aren't you? Here you are, then," he told me, "safe as houses. Have a pleasant night or day, sir, as the case may be."

Upstairs, by the light of the corridor, I found what I believe I had suspected I would find, and possibly even what I thought I should want to find—that Ann had left. I considered calling her room. I considered walking along the hall to her door and tapping it, again and again, until she opened. Instead, I stood in my doorway, turned the light switch on, and adjusted my glasses which, because of their tight-sprung new hinge, squeezed at my ear.

"Mr. Green," Lipsted said, "there are other medical conferences, I bet." He said it with the flippant generosity of minor characters in films and books who reunite the separated lovers.

"She's pretty much married," I said. "She has children. She has a cat and a dog."

"A passion thing," Schultz said. "Passion *and* a little epistemology on the side. That's not bad."

I asked for more coffee. Lipsted suggested a sandwich and a drink. I thought of my armful of chocolates and soft drinks and crisps. I thought of Ann's mouth around a triangle of sandwich.

"And," Schultz reminded me as he placed the pen in a stiff brown envelope and sealed the gummed flap with richly moist repeated licks, "you got the Indian guy to do your chapter." Lipsted poured coffee and the porcelain chattered. One of them spoke about lunch while I thought of how I'd walked into the small, dark room and had switched the lights back on, and then had taken one step backward into the hot, narrow corridor to look and look at the messy bed, the empty room. As I thought of it again, I saw some stiff, exhausted passenger who didn't look like me. He had just walked over from Arrivals, and he didn't want to go inside yet. He waited, perhaps for the Great Southern staff who would make up the room from which Ann, and then I, had already checked out.

JACOB
MOLYNEUX

DESIRE LINES

I was exposed. He had crept up behind the bush. I'd thought I was invisible. Then that hard grip came out of nowhere and dragged me straight back through the tangled branches. He seemed huge, irresistible. Now he yanked me to my feet, his fingers crushing my inner arm. I'd seen this cop before. He'd been out of uniform, but I remembered those blue eyes.

"Your luck just changed, little man," he said. He steered me ahead of him, away from the paths that led back to the rest stop, through the woods until we reached the strip of sunlight along the chain-link fence. He pushed me up against it, holding me there with the heel of his palm in the small of my back.

"How old are you?" he asked.

"Fifteen," I said, the metal printing a pattern into my cheek.

"Young ripe fruit. Some people go all the way to Bangkok for a taste. What's your name?"

"David."

"Well, David," he said, "what do you think I'm going to do?"

I didn't have an answer.

"I'll tell you what: anything I want. So you'd best hope I don't want some of this," he said, and smacked me once, hard, on the ass.

"I wasn't hurting anybody," I said.

"Not the point," he said. "Do you realize I could kill you and nobody would know who did it?"

"I know."

"I could screw you and then kill you and even if someone saw me he wouldn't say a thing. He wouldn't want to explain what he was doing in here. He wouldn't want to wreck his whole life by helping out some kid who'd already be dead by then anyway. Do you understand me?"

"Yes," I said.

"What did I just say?"

"You said you could kill me."

"I said nobody gives a shit what happens to you back here."

"I know."

"So what am I going to do? Come on, give it a try."

"I don't know," I said. He tugged my hands behind my back and I felt sharp cold steel encircle my wrists. I could feel it against the bone. I was still pinned against the fence and I couldn't turn and look at him. There was no one around. In front of me, through the fence, were the fields, full of sun-drunk grasshoppers, that led to the road home.

"Haven't you learned anything watching people sneak around these woods?"

"I'm not sure."

"Most of what you see in here doesn't even turn you on, does it? You don't even have that excuse."

"Not really," I admitted.

"You prefer girls, but you're too lazy to get off your ass and go find yourself one."

"You don't know anything about me," I said.

I had a scholarship to boarding school and when I came home in the summers I didn't have anything to do. My father had been dead since I was ten and we still lived in the same house, my mother working a series of teaching jobs in an attempt to keep up with the mortgage. We could always hear Interstate 80 and we were used to the sound. It was no different, most of the time, from living near a fast river. A convoy shifting up and humming along in the middle of the night was part of the weather of our dreams. But each time I came home after I'd been away at school I would notice it as if for the first time, and for a few days feel a constant low-grade irritation.

We lived on a dead-end road parallel to the highway, which was about three hundred yards away across a tangle of fallow fields and swampy ground. But I never thought much about the fact that we lived so near a rest stop until my mother sent me a clipping one winter about a pack of wild dogs that had ripped open the throats of a neighbor's sheep. Apparently the dogs had been left, one by one, at the rest stop out on the highway, and had banded together and gone hunting. They were dead now, the article said, all of them shot, and a fence had been put up behind the woods of the rest stop to turn back any new dogs that might be abandoned. I remember my mother wrote in her letter how sorry she felt for the dogs, yet how glad she was I'd been away at school, in case they might have run me down on my bike and mauled me.

I sat at a picnic table and watched people hurry for the bathrooms, fleeing cars and each other in a kind of frantic stupor. They checked the oil, walked dogs, picnicked, changed babies. They studied maps, popped pills, practiced tai chi, and kissed each other before switching drivers and heading west. I soon realized they thought I was one of them.

It gave me a sad feeling, knowing I could sit there all day and nobody would look twice. I had crossed the burr-ridden fields and the swamp, scaled the fence, traversed the woods, and now nothing. I was nothing. I watched a small old man walk a stiff-legged bulldog along the grass between the bathrooms and the woods, and as he came closer I rose to meet him. I squatted in front of the dog, rubbed its skull between the bulging eyes, looked up at him, and said, "Nice dog. Does he like to drive?"

"It's easier for her since she went deaf," he said.

"That's terrible."

"She don't complain."

"No, I guess not." I didn't know what to say next. There was a long pause. Finally, he helped me out, though I could see he wasn't interested.

"Where you heading?" he asked.

"New York City," I said. "We got a tip my runaway sister might be there."

"You'd best tell your parents they're driving the wrong way," he said. "This is the westbound side of the highway."

"Yes, I know," I answered quickly, feeling myself blush. "The thing is, my mother left her purse at the Burger King twenty miles back. I told her it's probably gone by now but we're going back to look anyway."

"Bad luck all round," he said, and gave me a quick hard look.

"Not really. It's not as bad as it sounds." I had no idea what this meant, but I guess it tipped his scales because he turned abruptly away, and his dog toddled after him.

I went home soon after that, cursing my stupidity. But I'd broken the ice, and I was back the next day.

I had learned I was a bad liar. This time I was more patient. I went into the rest rooms and washed my hands beside a man who was ferociously brushing his teeth before the mirror. He was foaming at the mouth, staring himself down. I dried my hands under a blower and sauntered outside, stretching, pretending to myself I was stiff from hours of travel. I bought a soda from a machine, and stopped to study a map. There was a red circle on it, with the words *You are here.* Walking on, I saw a Winnebago with little metal stairs leading up to an open door in the side, and as I passed I caught a glimpse of a small girl sitting cross-legged in the gloom, watching a tiny TV. She turned her head to look at me, and her glasses reflected the blue light of the TV. I wanted to go up those steps, hide with her, but I did not stop. I felt giddy and intensely aware, even the fingertips at my sides pulsing, testing some nuance in the hot sunlight. The smell of cut grass was rich, almost overpowering.

A young couple was picnicking on the hood of their pale green Plymouth Valiant. I sat down nearby and watched them use a pocketknife to cut slices of salami and cheese. They tore hunks of bread from a round loaf. I saw her split an orange's skin with her teeth, peel it, and feed him slices. His hair was slicked back and he wore one of those gas-station shirts with somebody else's name stitched across the breast. A chain hung in a loop at his waist. She had choppy short black hair and sunglasses and a tank top that showed off a tattoo on her shoulder. They had Georgia plates, peach colored.

When they finished they lit cigarettes and she leaned against the car while he lolled up against her, his elbow on the roof, saying things that made her tuck her chin against her chest and smirk. He whispered in her ear, ran his lips down her neck and kissed the tattoo—I couldn't see what it was—on her shoulder. His palm was on her abdomen, moving in slow circles. She leaned her head back and blew a long stream of smoke and then pushed him away. A moment later they had stored their food and were heading across the grass, arm in arm, toward my bench. They passed by without looking at me. When they reached the woods they loitered along the edge until they reached an opening. Then they ducked quickly out of sight. I got up to follow them.

Up against the fence, handcuffed, smelling the sweet grass cooking in the sunlight, feeling the heat on the backs of my pants, on my shoulders and hair, a certain somnolence settling over my limbs replacing fear and anger even against my will—I was helpless. He still had his palm pressed against my back, though I wouldn't have been able to rouse myself to run if he'd let me go.

"My father knows I'm here," I said.

"Bullshit."

He was right. Nobody knew where I was. The sun grew heavier against my back. I couldn't think clearly, and my breath was shallow. His hand left my back and I felt weightless, as if a breeze could make me shimmer and sway.

"You said I don't know you," he said, his voice calmer now. "What don't I know?"

"Nothing," I said. "I was wrong."

"There must be something I need to know."

"There isn't anything."

"What about *me*?" he asked. "What do you know about me?"

"I don't know anything," I said.

"You don't know anything. But you weren't afraid I'd catch you. You didn't even think about it."

I felt his hands reach around my waist and unbutton my jeans. He hooked his fingers inside the waistband and yanked my pants and underwear to my knees. I had never felt so naked.

I closed my eyes and saw how I must look, face against fence, pants at my knees, handcuffed.

"We have names for people like you," he said. "Peeping Toms. Voyeurs. Watchers. Have you heard of them?"

"I think so."

"It doesn't take very much imagination, now does it?"

"I wasn't hurting anyone," I said. He didn't answer. The grasshoppers buzzed. Several minutes passed. He was silent and seemed to have followed this line of interrogation to some kind of conclusion, but I knew he wasn't gone. I was afraid and I wanted him to say something. I didn't care what. I could hear the highway, faintly, and far away there were voices.

Park rangers call them "desire lines," those unplanned paths worn gradually into the earth through some collective focusing of intention, some desire to connect point A to point B in a more direct, pleasing way. Sometimes such paths, thousands of years old, help archaeologists reconstruct the lives of vanished civilizations. They posit former sites of water where the paths end, or map the routes an essential prey followed on its yearly migrations. Many, I imagine, are never explained. Beside the highway, behind the rest stop, paths forked through the woods, narrow paths veering suddenly from the main artery, some of them subtle, guarded by low branches, indicated only by the trace electricity from a stranger's quick intuition or relentless need, others littered with cigarette butts and trash, even the leaves soiled and tired.

I didn't know which way the couple had gone. Inside the woods the sun hit the smooth brown layer of dead leaves in blinding white patches surrounded by a cool and shadowy light. I'd passed through these woods on the way to the rest stop but I hadn't thought to linger, hadn't known the extent of the network of paths. The Georgia couple had vanished and I didn't want to go rushing loudly through the undergrowth in pursuit. But I wanted to find them and this made me a hunter. The quiet heightened my concentration as I padded along the hard dirt of the central artery, peering through layers of trees and past clumps of rhododendron bushes that had been planted in some long-gone time. I was startled when a man in a white oxford shirt came toward me in the opposite direction, his eyes locked on mine until he passed, seeming to deliberately brush my hip with his own. When I looked over my shoulder I saw he had stopped and was still staring at me in an aggressive way that seemed to demand some response. I didn't understand what this man had to do with me, but he was neatly dressed, short, balding, and paunchy, and I suspected he'd come back here to walk around, relax a little, and had thought I was disturbing the peace. I was guilty of something and he seemed to know what it was. To shake the almost palpable touch of his gaze I took a less worn path to the left and plunged past a series of rhododendron bushes until I stopped, listening, looking for the white shirt, hearing nothing but the traffic, which sounded muffled and distant. I knew about psychopaths, but I was pretty sure this man didn't qualify.

The path began to merge with the undergrowth, but I studied the grasses and saw that in places they had been bent and crushed by passing feet. I went on. A cluster of ragged red mushrooms with pulpy white undergills was slowly disintegrating at the foot of a tree beside the path. I took a few careful steps and saw a used condom bleached and worn by time, sun, and rain. The nearer I bent to the ground, the more things seemed to leap out at me—another condom; a scrap of paper with a note written in blue ink, blurred to illegibility by moisture. Then a dense, gleaming rhododendron blocked the nearly invisible path. It frightened me, as if something were hidden inside, watching, and a sudden shiver ran through my body so that I turned and ran the short distance back to the main path. Then, fear becoming energy, possessing me with a kind of manic thoughtless motion, I hurried up every path I could find, leaping quickly and quietly over fallen branches, stopping to listen with the sixth sense of one who hunts and is hunted, rushing on, sometimes meeting another path that led back to the main one, sometimes retreating and trying another.

I found them at the far end of the last path, one overgrown by thorny blackberry bushes that left painful red scratches on my arms and hands. They were off the path about fifteen yards. His hands were under her bare thighs, which were wrapped around his waist so that she did not touch the ground as with linked fingers she held the back of his neck and bent her torso backward as if trying to pull him to the ground, while he clenched his teeth and fought her drag with all his strength.

I watched, and then I backed slowly away because I was sure they would soon feel my devouring eyes on their flesh. I walked aimlessly now, or so I thought, letting my feet carry me until I had returned to the looming rhododendron at the end of the first path, circled it, dropped to my hands and knees, parted the branches, and crawled inside. The light was green and it smelled sweet and cool. What do adolescent boys do? Well, I did *that* right away—making my hand her hand as I faintly implored her to stop, warned her that we might get caught.

"Where do you live?" asked the cop. He was behind me but he wouldn't let me see him.

"Across these fields," I told him, watching a distant hawk in a rough current tilt and bump up, down, up, then soar quickly, vertically as if lifted on a string. I pressed my brow hard against the metal fence to distract myself from the dull ache in my shoulders and the awful sensation of metal on bone. "If you let me go I promise I won't come back," I said.

"Who do you live with?"

"My mother," I said, sensing that if I lied he would know immediately. "But I'm away most of the year," I added. "I don't really live here anymore."

"Just passing through on business, huh?"

"No. I go to boarding school."

"Where's your father?"

"He's dead."

"Who killed him?"

"Who?" I said. "He killed himself."

"Sorry to hear that," he said, and for a moment he was not taunting me. "I really am."

"It was a long time ago," I said, my voice neutral, but right away I felt something rise in my throat and I had to swallow it back.

"You're a tough one," he said.

"Let me go. Please," I said, thinking my disclosure had won me some leverage.

"Hold your horses, David. I happen to like looking at your ass."

"Please," I begged. "At least let my hands go."

"I can't do that. I just can't," he said. I felt his breath on my neck. "Listen. Why don't *you* tell *me* why I should let you go? What have you got to offer the world besides a cute ass, bad luck, greedy eyes, and a death wish?"

It's true I watched.

There was the nervous man with the stolen purse, and the father who backed his son against a tree and kept poking him in the chest as he told him he'd better start behaving or he'd wind up in the hospital like last time. There was the grandmother in a McDonald's uniform who swigged three tiny bottles of rum in quick succession, put a fresh piece of gum in her mouth, and hurried back up the path. There were peaceful people who strolled through the woods breathing deeply, bending their stiff necks, running fingers over the bark of trees and the translucent leaves of ferns.

One day I saw two men standing a few feet apart, staring at each other's genitals as they ferociously pumped their hands up and down. I sat very still in my cave, and I felt as if I were watching two cruel gladiators. They seemed violent and grotesque, exemplars of contortion and speed, performers of some supremely masculine ritual. The taller one had astonishingly blue eyes. His face hung slack and expressionless and the Adam's apple rose and fell in his strong neck as if he were continually swallowing back the full extent of his desire. They didn't touch each other, neither said a word, and when they finished—in less than a minute—left separately.

Such spectacles provided rare punctuation, shaping long sentences of solitude and quiet.

But what I remember with feeling is that green light and clean rich smell of soil, the stiff, shining, almost black leaves fanned like daggers between the outer world and my thoughts. What I remember is lying on my side, drifting with slit eyes while somewhere it rained and water ticked slowly earthward from leaf to leaf and flocks of small black birds journeyed with quick swoops through the green gloom. The world grew still and bounded, no larger than the woods, and I listened then for the footsteps of my father, wondering what I would do when he appeared, whether I would show myself, and how I would do it, what I would find to say—or if I'd merely watch his face to find that he was never worth my love.

I was not inventive. I took no photographs, built no secret tunnels, installed no shelves, wrote no messages to post to trees for strangers' eyes. I was inert, vegetative, ruminant. I didn't come every day because I didn't want to use up my spot, wear it out, but anticipation of the next visit suffused everything else I did that summer.

Sometimes I fell asleep, dreaming voices that I woke to find were real. And once I slept through dusk and opened my eyes in darkness. I lay still. I didn't know what time it was. I was chilled and it felt like the middle of the night. I could hear cars and trucks chasing each other's taillights west and I imagined the drivers' dark silhouettes, their faces lit faintly, brutally from below by dashboard lights.

Frozen, I listened for footsteps. My mind began to open to the cascading night. I thought of how near I was to the poorly lit parking lot and the concrete building with its rows of black empty toilet stalls. Then my terror blossomed, its architecture jagged and intricate as crystal—I pictured myself locked inside that building, and because I was shivering I could feel the bathroom's cold tile floor as if I were actually standing on it barefoot, the mirror above the sink reflecting a slash of moonlight, and in its gray depths a small figure approaching. . . .

I clawed my way out of the bush and ran, my arms in front of me to ward off branches, my eyes squinted and head lowered. I could feel someone behind me, just missing my leg as I scaled the fence, gaining as I fled through dark fields, stumbled on pitted ground and left one sneaker in low-lying muck, teeth reaching for my heels as, scratched, burred, I chased the endlessly withdrawing lights of our house that flickered in and out of sight behind a windbreak.

I reached the road, slowed to a fast walk for the last stretch. My mother was burning kilowatts, even the lawn illuminated by the light flowing from the house. I could see her through the window, sitting at the kitchen table, reading a novel. I knew she was waiting for me, that she had been worried when she didn't find me at home when she returned from her afternoon of teaching at a community college an hour away. I was still breathing hard, but now, seeing her alone in the house as she was during the long winters when I was away at school, I knew that whatever I had been afraid of was not what she feared for me, not wild animals or mass murderers, but something else I could never find a way to speak of in her presence. Something I carried in myself that would drive me back to those woods the next day, and finally drive me on from there to ever finer palaces of loneliness. That was twenty years ago. I have long since joined the tribe of those far from home, driving through, numbed and taunted by the endless flicker of passing landscapes. With each year the lines of desire cross and recross, gradually darkening the entire map.

I went inside, knowing she would neither question nor believe my lies.

I saw the tall blue-eyed man a second time a week after the first. He came rapidly down the path, followed in a few seconds by an equally tall and powerful white-haired man who was dressed like he was about to tee off at the country club.

They faced each other and neither made a move. Then the older man took several bills out of his wallet and rolled them up. He stepped forward and slid these into the younger man's front pocket. Then he produced a white handkerchief and carefully unfolded it on the ground, lowered himself on one knee and then the other, and opened the other's pants. The younger man had not moved, and now he turned his head to the side and spat, then held out a closed fist, which he opened in front of the kneeling man's face to reveal a condom.

"Thank you," said the white-haired man, as if he'd been afraid to ask for it himself. He used his teeth to open the wrapper. A shock of gray hair fell across his eyes but his concentration never wavered. The blue-eyed man was facing me as he stood there, and for a moment he looked right at the bush, right at my eyes. I was sure he couldn't see me, but even so, it was unnerving, and I was glad when they finished and left.

And so the next day, as I have said, his powerful hand got me in a pincer hold and dragged me into the light. He was on duty, and now I was up against the fence bare assed and he wanted to know what I could offer the world. But I couldn't think of anything. I didn't know what he wanted me to say, what anyone could offer the world. All I could think of was getting to the other side of that fence and never coming back. There were many other questions he could have asked, questions I would have tried to answer with all my heart: Tell me about your father. Do you miss him? What was he like? How did he die? (The report in the local paper had quoted the driver of the truck that hit him: "He was walking along the shoulder and just as I got to him he veered sharply to his left. It was the quickest move I've ever seen. It was just like a halfback diving for the end zone.")

The blue-eyed cop wasn't interested.

"Nothing?" he asked, and I heard the sound of a buckle opening. "Nothing to offer?" he repeated, and I heard the belt slide through fabric and come loose with a *whoosh.* I wanted him to ask about loneliness, and all my secret desires. About waiting, and stillness, and nightmares. I wanted to say: Let me go—I have suffered enough in this short life. But he didn't see the point in any of that. And for an instant I heard the whistle of the future as it swung through the air.

TIM GAUTREAUX

RODEO PATROL

Four inmates walked out into the hot, powdery dirt of the corral to sit in folding chairs at a neon-orange card table. Jimmy, the burglar, was the youngest, a tall, bent rail of a man with scrambled-egg hair and a barbecued, narrow face. Where he dragged his boots, the soil smoked. He didn't want to sit at the table under the blowtorch sun with his palms down on the flimsy surface, waiting for the pain, but the others had told him that if he stayed with them longest, if they all could just sit there with their hands on the table while it happened, they could win, and the reporters would put their pictures in the statewide paper where the parole board would see what good eggs they were, competitors, brave winners. Two members of last year's winning team were free already.

Minutes before, Jimmy had leaned inside the rough-cut

fence and watched what had happened to the other teams. The first foursome to compete had tried not to look. They were veterans. He had watched Red Tex, the dope dealer, and Black Diamond and Mollyfish and Ray-Ray sit like statues in a tornado, as though no kind of movement could save them. He'd looked and tried to be like them, draining himself of feeling as he heard the knock of the wood latch, the explosion of breath from the animal, and the ground-trembling plants of the hooves as the bull came on, but he'd turned his head from the arena at the first yell, which was followed by a sympathetic *Awwww* from the crowd. Three men had scattered, Red Tex was rolling on the ground, gored, and the card table had not come down yet. Two trusties came out with a stretcher and carried Red Tex away, passing by the fence where Jimmy stood and looked into the bloody man's face, which bore an expression saying, *It finally happened and I'm not surprised one damned bit.*

Now Jimmy was in the arena waiting for the bull to arrive like a decision come out of thin air. Nookey, a hairless older man, who was in for dynamiting a toxic waste dump, sat across the table. "Okay," he said. "Look at it like this. It's like a judge saying something and you can't stop it or change it."

Little Claude, an accordionist who had burned down his wife's lover's house, nodded agreement. "Don't look at that judge, don't look at that bull," he said, spreading his palms out on the plywood. The fourth was a new man, a murderer who would never get out, not even after death, for no family would claim him and someday he would be laid in the prison graveyard by the swamp. He was big, with a head of thick black hair combed back and eyes as full of wild instinct as a bear's, a man whom a stupid woman would notice and love at once.

Jimmy spat, and his spit sat on top of the dust like quicksilver. "Red Tex's group has the best time. Ray-Ray picked up his hands right before the bull hooked."

"Let's don't talk about it," Little Claude said. "If you talk about it, you gonna try to get out the way. You gonna pick up your hands."

Nookey closed his eyes just for a moment. "We got to be still and hope he goes for the table."

"This is something," the murderer said, and the other men looked at his eyes, which were open too wide for the strobe-hot sun, as though they were blind and unaffected by light. He had the worst position. His back was to the gate, and behind him a prison guard gave a Brahma repeated shocks with a cattle prod, the animal shrieking and trying to climb the boards.

Jimmy turned to the murderer. "Why you doing this? We can get out."

"I can get out," said the murderer.

"You doing over three hundred years, man," Nookey said, tilting the white dome of his head so sweat could roll off sideways, missing his eyes. "They welded the door on you."

"I can get out," he said again, looking at nobody.

A little cloud passed over, and the table turned dark.

The men looked at their hands on the dusty surface. When the cloud cleared the sun, the orange wood glowed like hot iron, and when Jimmy heard the gate latch knock open, the wood under his hands filled with fire.

The bull spun out of the pen like a tornado of angry meat, a gray animal with black, shadowed eyes, a lurching hump on his back, and under him, his tortured, swinging bag loaded with electricity from the shock sticks of the howling guards. His hooves kicked up the floury dust, and it seemed for a moment that he had camouflaged the men and their bright table, that the onion eyeballs would not turn on them and the animal would not bolt into their quiet pocket of territory. Jimmy felt the dirt under his boot soles jump each time the animal planted a hoof, but he looked at nothing and willed his mind empty, waiting for whatever fact was about to be proved on him. He saw Nookey's face go blank, Little Claude's lids close. The murderer's eyes got even wider and he looked over at the bull. "Easy," Jimmy said in his direction.

"Easy," the murderer repeated, with no inflection. Jimmy saw the man's black hair gleam, every strand in place in soft oiled lines like the hair on holy statues, and then the bull whirled and jumped for them, its haunches digging in, its sea of angry muscles directed at something it sought without knowing why, choosing the table and the men as a target with the logic a thunderbolt uses to select a tree or a house or a man walking along with a rake hoisted on his shoulder.

The animal could choose, if they sat still enough, to go

for the table, to come in beside one of them and put a horn on the underneath, or even its whole head, and give it a murderous heave out of their hands. If they all kept their palms down, they would do better than Red Tex's team. Or the Brahma could choose to lay his skull against the table's edge, and then it would go hard for the man on the other side. Or he might lay the barrel of a horn against a man and push them all down like bowling pins. None of the men thought any of this; they were not there, as far as Jimmy could tell. They had drained themselves of feeling and were white and empty.

What the bull did do was lower his head and hit Nookey from the rear, the animal's flat skull battering the chair and the man's backbone together, shoving his chest against the table that shocked into Jimmy's ribs, the plywood top breaking in two and heaving up in the middle. Little Claude raised his hands right before a horn tip went through his cheek and into his mouth. Jimmy's long arms cracked like a whip over his head when the table hit him, and then he was in the dust watching a hoof come down next to his face. Two rodeo clowns fell off the fence and distracted the animal as Little Claude dragged Jimmy clear into an opened gate, and a trusty hustled a white-faced Nookey over the fence, where he was put down in fresh manure, his legs kicking as a man with a cross on his shirt-sleeve knelt down to blow breath into his flattened lungs. The clowns got to the pen where Jimmy lay, jumping in ahead of the bull, and then Jimmy looked under the bottom board to see the murderer, whom everyone had seemed to forget, sitting untouched in front of nothing, his hands still out flat, palms down, in the center of the ring, his hair flawless, his eyes open. Jimmy wanted to yell, but there was no air in him. The rodeo announcer said something incomprehensible and awful, a squawk of speech, and before the clowns could get back over the fence, the bull ran into the murderer like a train, hitting him so hard that rivets flew out of the folding chair.

Jimmy lay back and took his share of the atmosphere in little sips until he could breathe again. He saw arms come under a board and drag out the murderer's body. After a minute or two, a guard holding a shock stick climbed into the pen with Jimmy and told him that Red Tex's group had won the competition.

"That right?"

"They gonna get their pictures in the paper," the guard told him. He looked at Jimmy as though he almost felt sorry about something. "We can only have one winner."

"Well," Jimmy said, looking under the bottom board to where the bull was trying to kill a clown trapped in a barrel, "maybe so."

JOYCE CAROL OATES

THE PHOTOGRAPHER

THOUGH PRIMITIVE PEOPLE FEAR THAT THE CAMERA WILL STEAL THEIR SOULS, THE TRUTH IS THAT ONLY THE CAMERA, SKILLFULLY EMPLOYED, PROVIDES US WITH WHAT "SOULS" WE HAVE.

—from *The Actor's Handbook and the Actor's Life*

"Do as I say. Don't freeze."

He was tall, slope shouldered, bone thin. She would have estimated his height at six feet two or three inches. His age?—not-young, but he had the alertness and arrogance of youth. His skin was the hue of a photograph negative, bumpy and pockmarked; he had a shrewd hawk face, with hooded eyes and a drooping left eyelid. In the harsh overhead light of the dope room Norma Jean could see a row of near-invisible serrated scars across his forehead at the hairline. His teeth, bared in a smile, were uneven and green-tinctured. He wore black, like a magician or a priest: a baggy black pullover jersey, black trousers that emphasized his pencil-legs, black canvas shoes splotched with chemical stains. His thinning, dyed-looking black hair grew shaggy and uneven past his ears; grizzled tufts sprouted from his ears like wires. *The ugliest man! Yet I could not look away.*

On a sling around his neck The Photographer was toting a bulky camera, and hanging from one shoulder a soiled duffel bag crammed with equipment. When Norma Jean saw the camera she instinctively froze. She was positioned behind an airplane fuselage, a canister of dope in both hands, and it was her naive belief that The Photographer had not only not seen her immediately, as any predator sights his prey, within seconds of stepping into the room, but that he wouldn't see her if she remained very still, crouched half in hiding.

His voice was a surprise, hoarse and oddly boyish, playful. "Ladies, hel-lo. I see you are all ladies—gurls—almost! Did they tell you I was coming? Well, my name is"—he paused slyly, smiling his aggressive smile—"hell, my name don't matter none. I'm a freelance photographer in the hire of *The Stars and Stripes* and I'm here on a pat-riotic mission to take 'morale-boosting' pitch-urs for the boys overseas." He meant to be funny and so most of the workers laughed, except Norma Jean, who heard only mockery and meanness in the man's voice. Why would a photographer say "pitch-urs" except he had some grudge against his assignment? His subjects? All the while he'd been speaking, his eyes were darting coldly about the room, assessing.

Norma Jean thought, *No! Not me.*

Yet a part of her was shivering in anticipation. For why would the Dark Prince come to this hellish place except for *her*?

There were twenty-seven workers in the dope room that morning, of whom six were men. The women were of varying ages, Norma Jean the youngest and a gray-haired grandma the eldest, in her sixties. What a flurry! What excitement! The women were touching their hair, glancing down in dismay at their stained coveralls, licking their lips self-consciously. Did they want their photographs taken by a stranger? But were they looking their best? A few of the younger women protested, couldn't he come back the next morning, but The Photographer waved his spidery fingers and told them to continue working, ignore him, he'd just walk around and have a look-see. He told them to think of him as invisible—"like God who sees all, loves all, and forgives all." But The Photographer's manner wasn't loving or forgiving, rather more impatient and dissatisfied as if he wanted to be anywhere but in the dope room at Radio Plane Aircraft trying not to gag at the smell. Norma Jean crouched at the far end of the row of fuselages, which were laid out like torsos on a dissecting table, saw that, in profile, The Photographer's upper spine had a bump in it, like his broken nose. He was walking now with an exaggerated military posture as if to forestall his vertebrae collapsing like dice. *So ugly! And mean. Yet I could not look away.*

With the sinister ungainliness of a predator bird forced to use its legs, not its wings, The Photographer circled the room. Once, twice. His sharp eye discovered only two or three females who merited the attention of his camera. One of these was a flirty, wide-hipped, red-haired girl in her twenties, and with this girl he exchanged wisecracks as he took her picture *click! click! click!* asking her to remove her scarf and she blushed saying her hair wasn't "nice enough" and he drawled, "Red, your hair is your 'nicest' feature, it sure is," but so smoothly you wouldn't have thought it was meant to be hurtful, and maybe it wasn't. Her heart pounding hard, Norma Jean was edging around the fuselage hoping he hadn't noticed her. Well, she'd seen that he had noticed her—he'd even winked at her (had he?) but she'd looked quickly away and made her face go dead, dead, dead. The sight of a camera in a man's hands reminded her of something she wanted to forget.

The Photographer spent some time posing another girl beside the fuselage, hands on her hips, commanding her to smile, smile, smile, until her face was distended like a cartoon face, then abruptly he changed his mind, lowered his camera, and said in a flat voice, "Honey, this'd be a total waste of time for us both. Back to work." The girl tried to laugh, standing there looking as if she'd been slapped in the face. The Photographer's rudeness was becoming sharper with every minute.

Next, he stalked Norma Jean. Winking again, as if he'd been aware of her all along. "You, honey. You-with-the-dishwater-curls. Let's have a smile, pul-*ease.* If you love your country." His manner was Groucho Marx crossed with W. C. Fields. That humor you can't trust especially if you're a woman. Because to such a man the very idea *woman* is funny. Mutely Norma Jean shook her head, looking away and frowning. She'd been feeling dazed all that morning in the dope room, couldn't seem to shake her head clear, now trying to recall how she'd navigated her way through the corridors of Van Nuys High with certain of the guys staring at her and the bolder ones making remarks but she couldn't remember and anyway those had been only just kids and The Photographer was an adult man. And something more than an adult man. He was saying, cajoling, "Your boss gave me permission, y'know. 'Carte *blanche.*' " There was an edge to his voice that meant he'd begun to enjoy this, now he had a challenge; he liked a little resistance, instead of females eager to be photographed now a female playing coy with the camera. Norma Jean tried to disguise the scared-hurt look in her eyes she knew attracted men but The Photographer saw. "Honey, this is in the pat-riotic cause. Those lonely boys overseas. Y'know what lonely boys are like. Maybe you're married to one? They need their pinups. They want to see who's making the bomber planes they're flying so when they climb into one of these big babes—Va-Va-VOOM." The Photographer made a fierce gesture with his left fist that might have been obscene or only just playful depending upon your frame of mind. Norma Jean blushed, backing away and biting her lower lip. Hoping this hawk-man would think there was something wrong with her mentally, and leave her alone.

But there was no escape. The foreman was nowhere in sight. Norma Jean was The Photographer's prey, and he wasn't going to relinquish her. An avid, hungry light came up in his eyes and even the droopy lid of his left eye quivered. He was sighting her through the viewer. "Do as I say. Don't freeze. It's no accident I'm here. They directed me here to *you.* 'We got just the girl for you,' the plant manager told me, as soon as I explained my mission, 'go on back to the dope room and you'll find her,' and I asked what's this special girl's name and he said, 'Hell, Mr. Photographer, that girl don't need no name wearing a coverall with an ass like that. You can't miss her.' " This was said in a low cajoling-caressing voice for only Norma Jean to hear but Norma Jean refused to hear. Her co-workers had returned to their work and she was left alone nearly backed into a corner. She was frightened, confused. She saw that The Photographer wasn't so tall as she'd imagined, not much taller than her own height of five feet eight. He was clicking the camera, his gray-tinctured face now more livened, and his lips loosening into a truer, boyish smile. Almost, Norma Jean could have believed that he liked her. "Y'know who my boss is at *The Stars and Stripes*? Ron Reagan." Norma Jean shook her head blankly. Reagan? The actor Ronald Reagan? A second- or third-rate Tyrone Power, Robert Taylor, Clark Gable. It was surprising to her that an actor like Reagan had anything to do with a military magazine. It was surprising to think that an actor could do anything real, at all. "Okay, honey, more to the side—good! But smile, pul-*ease.*" Norma Jean smiled, a quick scared smile with just her mouth. *Click, click.* " 'Tits, ass, and leg, man—that's your assignment,' says Ron Reagan. He's the putative editor but the fact is the dumb asshole can hardly read copy let alone edit, and he sure don't know shit what's going on. 'How'm I supposed to get *leg*, man, in an aircraft factory?' I asked the SOB. 'Y'think dames like Betty Grable are doing their shifts in *bathing suits* and *high heels*?' " Norma Jean was staring at The Photographer, at his grimacing face behind the bulky camera, not hearing this, or not absorbing it, flushed with hurt and insult and gathering anger yet a part of her on the brink of laughter for the man was funny, mean and dirty-minded and funny, such sexual hostility was at the core of the most powerful male humor and how futile to stiffen in opposition to such power if in some way you could align yourself with it. "Now, honeybun, stand over here," The Photographer said bossily, daring to reach out and tug Norma Jean by the arm, positioning her beside one of the fuselages, "and pick up that canister, whatever the hell it is, but don't spray the fucker!—just hold." Norma Jean saw that she was holding the canister, yet not as she'd been holding canisters for weeks; she seemed suddenly to have forgotten how to use it, and its bulk and weight surprised her. *Click, click, click.* The Photographer laughed. "This looks phony as hell, I love it. 'Girl defense workers' in *The Stars and Stripes,* nobody wants 'em to look *real.* Okay, now turn this way a little. *Smile.*" Norma Jean managed at last to speak in a whisper saying she had to go back to work, please let her alone now, but The Photographer, clicking away, didn't hear. "More of a smile, kid. More like you mean it. Like I'm the love of your pathetic little American-girl life." Norma Jean had no intention of smiling and yet—quick and sudden and startling to her, she was smiling. *Click, click!* The Photographer grunted approval. Almost, she was surprising him, it seemed. "Gr-eat. You're a natural. Now this side, let's see your bust, not bad, baby, not bad at all, can you kind of pull this down a little, what d'you call it, the 'bib'—make the belt tighter, like this," without waiting for Norma Jean to assent he adjusted her coverall, tightening the straps and the belt. "Head back, like that—hey, y'know your head's big?—movie stars all got freaky-big heads, did you know that?—chin tucked in, now hold, don't breathe, not bad, baby, not bad at all." Next, The Photographer pulled off her scarf and fluffed out her hair, his slightly sour, mildewy breath warm upon her face and his fingers deft and familiar and hard as steel. "Don't touch me!" Norma Jean cried, backing off. She was tempted to aim the liquid plastic spray at The Photographer—right in the eyes! He'd be blinded for life.

For a tense moment they stared at each other. Then the Photographer laughed, and wagged a forefinger at Norma Jean. "Better not, baby. Your bosses would toss you out on your pretty little ass, then where'd you be? We're on our last roll so let's make this good." He was breathing quickly as if he'd been running and was invigorated by the exercise if a little out of condition. He was watching Norma Jean with a curious kind of interest, not respect exactly but a kind of thoughtful regard. He advanced upon her and another time it seemed to her that he was much taller than she, looming over her, intimidating her with his power, which was a raw male power and yet something more, not-raw, sheerly will, intellect. She shrank from his touch and would wonder afterward why she hadn't pushed him away with all her strength, why she hadn't even resisted. Close up, his skin was bumpy and serrated as a rock surface and his eyes were oddly small, beady and deep-set in shadowy sockets. The chain of small scars on his forehead made her think of Jesus Christ, the crown of thorns on His forehead. "I said—let's make this good. You with me?" Without waiting for an answer The Photographer pulled Norma Jean away from the fuselage area and to a tall narrow window in one of the walls; this fifteen-foot window was layered in grime, opening onto an air shaft, emitting only a grudging, grimy light. Though its upper panes were always open, it was impossible to discern any fresh air coming through. The Photographer spoke urgently now, as if inspired. "What we're gonna do, baby, is have you turn your face up, like this, and *smile.* Not grin, *smile.* Like you're gazing up at a clear blue sky and Jesus Himself is smiling down at you from a cloud 'cause you're so damn pretty, and your ass in coveralls is so damn sweet. Jesus is thinking He'd like another chance at being a man. Um-*hmmm!* Hee-*haw!* Jesus is thinking He fucked up pretty bad, the first time around." The Photographer raised his bulky camera and clicked the shutter, murmuring in his hoarse, mock-cajoling, caressing voice, "This is for the servicemen to see, baby. Real dreamy-like. Like you're waiting for them to come home, sweet little ass and all." *Click, click.* Norma Jean was gazing up at the air shaft, which was twilit at midday. The tension in her spine and chest had drained from her, strangely; as if it had been sucked from her and into The Photographer. How excited he was, how pleased with her; and how easy for her to please him. *All you need to do, really, is stay out of their way.* The Photographer was saying, murmurous as love-making, "Umm-*hmmm!* You're a natural, for sure. Maybe your nose is a little too long and kinda bunchy at the tip and your face is round as a dinner plate and skin's mushy looking as white bread, no bones beneath like a true classic beauty—Greta Garbo, say. And your hair's that shit-dish-water-blond. But the ass is good, the ass is real good, and the bust, and you're in good condition, impressive muscle tone for a female, like maybe you work out? lift weights? exercise like a guy? You're only a kid, right? Gonna be a kid all your life. Or maybe you won't live long. I see you're married, eh? Getting screwed regularly? But he's gone off, eh? Overseas? Screwing Polynesian girls, Malaysians, slant-cunts like slant-eyes, if he can get them? Hubby's gonna bring the clap home, honey. I'd be careful of hubby. Bet he's big, brawny, got a prick like a baton. Hubby's been cutting off Jap ears in the jungles and jamming bayonets up native female cunts, he ain't gonna tolerate American-style prissiness in bed, baby, take my advice. I've been covering every war for *The Stars and Stripes* since, hell—the Civil War. The War of 1812. I'm the official U.S. photographer. War's a lot of laughs, you bet. 'Morale boosting' is my job. What the sucker-servicemen have to keep them going is little girls like you. 'Tits, ass, and leg'—that's too much to ask? Hadn't better be! Can't win a war without something to win it *for.* Just like Schopenhauer said, ol' Arthur the 'Great Pessimist,' but he sure hit the nail smack on the head, life laughs at the individual's death, life is sheer unmitigated suffering, only illusion saves us, de-lusion, 'tits, ass, and leg'—*that's* the prize! *You're* the prize, baby. And, baby, you are *good.*"

Abruptly then it was over. The last *click!* of the shutter, the end of the roll of film, and the ordeal was over.

In all The Photographer had spent only twenty minutes with Norma Jean. Yet it seemed like hours. Flatly he said, "Okay, baby. See you in the funny papers."

He left her standing at the grimy window dazed with exhaustion, glassy eyed. She hadn't even realized he was gone. He hadn't told her his name—had he? Hadn't asked her name. A few yards away her co-workers were spraying dope as if nothing had happened. The women would be chilly with Norma Jean, stiff and disliking her, but they hadn't much liked her before. She wanted to cry, so humiliated! She felt used, like a tissue. Crumpled and tossed away.

THOMAS BELLER

CALLER I.D.

Panic at the video store. Two minutes to closing, and no decision. Several minutes of standing shoulder to shoulder with Alex in front of the new releases had yielded nothing, and so they split up. She paused in front of Classics, and before she could even decide what decade she might be interested in visiting, he returned clutching a box, looking pleased and, she thought, a little cruel, as if this was going to be a movie that would somehow edify and enrich her, as opposed to making her happy.

"Have you ever seen this?" he asked. He held it up.

"No," she said. "I haven't." She wanted to add that there was a reason she hadn't seen it, which was that she wasn't that interested in the Vietnam War.

"Closing," yelled the clerk. They both turned to look at him. He was an avid hockey fan. This, she felt, detracted greatly from the cinema-appreciating vibe of the store. He glowered at them in his blue Rangers jersey.

It was a chilly autumn night and the wind was gusting. He pulled her along brusquely, his arm around her shoulder, and she ducked her chin into the collar of her coat. One hand held the collar against the bridge of her nose, the other was pressed deep into her pocket, balled up in a fist. The short walk to her house made her long for the couch, and when they finally arranged themselves there, she felt a great sense of relief, as though everything up to that moment had been preparation. Now, on the couch, indoors, the night could begin, and their distinct, hardened, separate bodies could relax, commingle, and begin to entwine.

She was in her underwear and a T-shirt, with black socks pulled up over her calves. Her work clothes were in a pile on a nearby chair. Alex was still in his jeans, a T-shirt, and work boots.

The one unfortunate aspect to the situation, from Melissa's point of view, was the video: *Apocalypse Now.* Other than a brief shot of Martin Sheen's bare ass, she was finding it a bit abstract. But she knew that he wanted her to like it, so she leaned into his shoulder, pulled her feet under her, and watched. She could feel the warmth of his chest. He was a warm person, literally.

They had been together nine months. In the beginning they went out often. There was something exhibitionist about their ventures into the world together, as though they wanted to show each other off, and to revel in their newfound status as one half of a pair. But lately they'd been spending more and more time at home, *her* home. She had made an effort to make her living space accommodating and pleasant; it was soft edged, pillow strewn, and a bit peach in atmosphere and color. His place was either barren or pristine, depending on how you looked at it, and their time there was a bit like time in a motel room—exciting, theatrical, and alienating.

Then the phone rang, and Melissa cocked her head at the sound of it, not wanting to walk the ten steps into the kitchen and wanting with equal measure not to subject one of her friends to the humiliation of babbling into a machine while the two of them listened.

"I'll get it," she said in the middle of the second ring, and got up from the couch.

"Do you want me to press pause?" said Alex.

"No, I'll just be a second," she said.

The voice on the phone belonged to Rodney Donoghue. It took her by surprise, and made her shiver. It was deep and low and much too intimate.

"Hello, Melissa, it's Rodney," he said. "I'm just calling to say hi, see how you are." He had a way of pronouncing the most innocent comments in a sordid, suggestive manner, as though he were stroking her ass while saying it. This sort of duplicity was, she had come to understand, his specialty—high-mindedness and cordiality providing a thin gloss on his weirdly obsessive and unpleasant nature. His faintly Southern accent was particularly useful in this obscuring cause.

"Hi," she said, and instinctively glanced at Alex to see if he had registered any anxiety, any falseness, in her voice. She thought she sounded shrill and self-incriminating, but Alex just stared at the screen, watching Martin Sheen sulk on a boat going up the Mekong River.

"I'm just calling because I've been thinking about our last conversation," Rodney said.

You mean the one where I said I didn't think you were behaving properly and that your behavior was in fact offending me and that I wanted you to stop touching me that way, she wanted to say.

"Uhm, yeah?" she said instead, and concentrated on the background noise—a faint hiss—trying to figure out if he was calling from his cell phone again. When he had last called she had talked with him merrily for an hour, feeling the peculiar liberation and freedom that comes with the implied distance of a phone conversation, only to have him blurt out: "I'm in a car right in front of your building. Why don't I just come up and we can continue this in person?" She had been so flustered by this that she agreed.

"I thought the conversation didn't really go the way it should have," he said now. "Which was unfortunate, given that we normally have such a fine rapport."

He was a television talk show host, of the high-brow variety. Rapport was his specialty. She had spent several years of her life concluding many of her evenings lying in bed and watching him nod intelligently at one important, fascinating, and powerful guest after another, interrupting them with penetrating questions and lulling her with his deep, comforting, and faintly paternal voice. Who could blame her for being excited when she met him at a party?

She had rehashed this line of thought many times—*Her Innocence at the Beginning.* They had met at the party for the New York Film Festival, where she worked as a publicist. She had placed numerous calls to his office reiterating the invitation at the instructions of her boss. So it was natural that she should introduce herself. They had chatted amicably and he had listened attentively and nodded as she spoke—just like he did on the show—and she had felt the particular thrill of that rapt, attentive expression he always bestowed upon his guests.

"You're a very intelligent and perceptive woman," he had said at one point. "I'm curious to hear suggestions you might have for people on my show." She was aware that he was flattering her. She didn't mind. She was flattered to be flattered.

"Uhm, I'm sort of watching a movie," she said now.

"Which movie are you sort of watching?" he said.

"*Apocalypse Now,*" she said.

"You can hit pause," he said.

She wanted to snap something rude and witty at him.

"I'm just going to watch the movie now," she said instead. "Why don't we speak later." This was as terse as she could be without being conspicuous.

"All right. I really wanted to say that I'd like to see you

again. I don't want there to be any awkwardness between us because of my last visit. I enjoy your company and also value your opinions. I'm doing a one-hour special on Rembrandt and I thought you could have some input, maybe even help produce. It's all very preliminary."

She was amazed to note her body stiffening a little as he said all this, as though she were a cat being stroked. Her intellect registered the falseness, but she had heard him utter so many words with that homespun Southern accent of his, addressing the guests on his show, that she was instinctively pleased to have such good company in being deceived. She flashed to another moment of weakness, when she had ushered him into her apartment, as though he were there all the time. In a sense he was. Something very similar to the figure that had stood before her had been in her apartment countless times before, but confined to the diameter of the television screen. It had been unsettling to have it before her in all its ungainly life-sized reality.

She remembered the weird way his body had occupied space in her apartment, sitting right there on the couch where Alex now sat. It was so strange to see Rodney there, in his suit and tie, smelling faintly of cologne. She didn't smell the cologne until he got near her, and right away she could picture him applying it, standing in the mirror and letting his face go slack with admiration while thinking: *Women love this smell, and they love me.*

He had said kind, intelligent words of praise to her, loosened his tie, and then he had put his hand on her thigh and stroked it. There was so much gross sexual energy in that single caress that she had almost allowed him to continue. The idea of letting this overly suave, self-possessed, attractive, and successful older man barge into her life and fuck her, thereby letting his already distorted ego pump even further out of shape at his success with her, was so repulsive that her mind froze in a kind of fascination when considering it. He stroked her thigh several times and moved closer. She was under a kind of spell. Fortunately, the cologne was nauseating. It was a metaphor for the whole situation. There was something rank, false, and toxic about this man. She slapped his hand away and asked him to leave.

"All right," she said now. "I'll talk to you soon." Her voice softened at the very end, as though to leave the door to Rodney open just a crack. She put the phone down, aware of her moment of duplicity.

She went back to the couch where Alex sat slouched, clutching the video remote, and, as she leaned back against him, was aware of how much she hoped he had noticed something. She wanted him to call her on it. He was always getting into moods and sulks. What she wanted from him was some rage, threat, and anger. She wanted action.

Alex, without looking at her, pressed rewind. Images flickered backward on the screen. A boat raced backward down a river, led by a man water-skiing backward.

"You missed some good parts," he said. "You should really see the whole thing straight through." He put his right arm around her, and casually pulled her against him.

"Who was that on the phone?" he asked nonchalantly.

"Jim Milford," she lied, citing an old friend from college who was familiar to Alex as Just a Friend. She was a terrible liar. Whenever she attempted it she tried to remember what she normally sounded like, and, drawing an utter blank, was forced to impersonate a self she couldn't imagine. The words slipped out and she glanced at his expression to see if there was a flicker of suspicion. She half hoped to find it.

There was nothing but Alex's slack television gaze, focused on the screen, and for a brief moment she hated him for his inertia even more than she hated herself for her gullibility. For a split second she considered blurting it all out but then decided that would be ridiculous. She hadn't done anything wrong. Besides, Alex hadn't earned a confession. She wasn't going to do all the work.

Alex kept his cool. There was nothing to be gained by expressing the intense pang of anger and fear that had shot through him when he heard her voice dip and observed her body twist slightly, turning away from him just before she put the phone down. And now this outlandish lie about who she'd been talking to, her voice trilling upward, her nostrils flaring, her desperate glance to see if he noticed. He had always cherished her sincerity and in a way he was touched by this transparency. But he was also furious, disgusted, frightened, and all the emotions that had been coursing through him for weeks were further inflamed by this new complication. He had come to see Melissa as the indispensable shock absorber between himself and the world. He sank into her house, her pillows, *her;* he experienced this as a narcotic, not as love. It removed him from life as opposed to bringing him closer to it. That was his fear, at least, coupled with the concern that he was becoming addicted to her. He felt the swell of fear that comes with dependence, as well as the resentment. He depended on her even for housing at this point. His own home was strange to him. It was a place where he changed socks. And even these had migrated to her fluffy apartment.

"Baby," he said, summoning the paternal, Big Daddy attitude he often assumed when he wanted her to calm down and do what he wanted. "This is a really good movie. You have to concentrate a little, but it's worth it."

"Okay, honey," she said. She looked into his eyes in that way of hers—trusting, sweet, soft, and open, but spiced with that tiny but fierce self-preserving instinct, within which, he thought, was the capacity for deceit. He admired that. He liked it when she was strong.

Then he remembered the betrayal he was sure he had just suffered, and was seized with a blinding desire to slap her across the face. He wanted it both ways. He had no idea what he wanted. In the midst of his confusion he was determined to be calm and bide his time.

He tried to resist the pleasures that the night had to offer—her kindness, softness, the sweetness of coupledom—but could not, and eventually, as sugar turns into energy, his anger and irritation transformed itself into lust. He began stroking her hair and kissing her neck. Their bodies melded into each other. She received his touches with a weird energy that stemmed as much from relief as from desire.

The sounds of a helicopter attack on a small Vietnamese village filled the room. At first he found captivating the juxtaposition of the sounds of love and war, then he grew distracted by it, and grappling for the remote, he hit the pause button and threw it on the floor with abandon. They started touching and kissing again and soon were having an amazingly desperate encounter on the couch, with his pants around his ankles. For some reason he liked doing it with his pants around his ankles. Then the pause automatically ended, and the movie picked up right in the middle of Robert Duvall walking around with his bastard expression and cowboy hat saying, "I love the smell of napalm. It smells like . . . victory."

"I don't believe it," he said, a little embarrassed, as though someone had in fact walked into the room. He had to grapple to find the remote control in order to turn the video off, and then a game show popped on the TV when the video went off, necessitating a frantic search for the other remote control to quell the horrible screams of game-show pleasure. By then there was almost nothing left.

"I'm being destroyed by technology," he feebly joked. For a while they just lay there next to each other, breathing. Gradually, they recovered, and began again. There was some nugget of panic and desperation in his chest—triggered by the frantic search for the remote controls, the brief attack of the shrieking game show, the hushed sound of her voice on the phone—but his insecurity made the sex better, as though he wanted to devour her and thereby be assured that no betrayal was forthcoming. At the end of it he noticed her cheeks were bright pink. He was never sure whether this actually meant something had happened, but he always took it as a personal triumph.

Afterward she went to the bathroom, and he stood, pulled his pants up, and went to the kitchen counter, where a gaggle of electronic devices was pushed into the corner—phone, answering machine, and a small white gadget she had recently purchased, caller I.D. This little white box registered the number of the person calling you, and his or her name, on a small LED screen. He hit the last-call button and a number popped up along with a name: *R. Donoghue.* What a clever little device, he thought.

She had told him it had been an impulse buy at Bed, Bath, and Beyond. "They had it right by the checkout counter and I thought what the hell, nineteen ninety-nine, it could be interesting," she had said. Perfect that a store specializing in the pleasures of the home and hearth, a place devoted to the comforts of couples, should have such a suspicious device stuck there as an afterthought, as though the hour or two their patrons had spent contemplating the pleasures to be had, using their fluffy white towels, cuddling in flannel sheets, cooking on immaculate Teflon, was the perfect setup for a pang of paranoia: What is really going on with the person with whom all this comfort is to be shared?

He stared at the number on the little gray screen. He heard the faint sound of a toilet flush, and like a shoplifter who stuffs something in his pocket without thought, only to feel a sense of shock at what he has just done and a simultaneous sense of its irreversibility, he picked up the phone and dialed the number. There was something perverted and treasonous about this gesture just after sex, this little bit of romantic espionage. But then he had been betrayed too. Or had he? He hovered on the edge of hateful seething feelings that, in all truth, had no real basis. And if he hung up right away, they never would. Some self-preserving instinct told him to do so; the part of him addicted to the soft warmth of her, the fluffy-towel loving part of him that wanted pleasure and comfort and softness in the world, told him to hang up and be done with it.

But there was another force within him, too, destructive and condemning, an Old Testament fire-and-brimstone force that said life should be hard, that wanted to punish.

She came into the room in her nightgown, a powder puff of loveliness. She gave him a mildly quizzical look when she saw him on the phone.

"Hello," came a voice after the second ring. "Hello?"

Alex nearly laughed at the obviousness of it. If one went to central casting and said, "We need a voice for the Other Man," this is what they would send over. It was ridiculous. The only weird thing was that there was something familiar about it. He looked at Melissa standing there, looking at him, and felt horrible at last. It was a kind of catharsis, to feel like such a shit that he no longer hated her, but himself; in feeling guilty toward her, he could cleanse himself of his anger toward her. He put the phone down in the middle of the third "Hello?"

"Do you want to watch the movie some more?" she asked. She was being accommodating.

"No, hon. That's fine." He went and hugged her.

"Who was that?" she said softly.

"My answering machine."

They got in her fluffy bed and cuddled. Then they rolled onto their backs and turned on the television. Alex stretched his left arm straight out and cracked his wrist. It was a brisk motion—the snap lent it an air of precision. Melissa had come to recognize this simple gesture as a sign that something was bothering him.

"What's wrong?" she said.

"Nothing," he said.

But she didn't believe him. She experienced that crack in the same way swimmers treading water in the ocean experience a strange bit of turbulence just beneath their toes, where the water is cold and dark.

He brought her close and held her. His moments of disgust with her were often followed by remorse and relief, as though only at the last moment had he stopped himself from smashing a precious object to the floor.

They held on to one another, flipped channels, browsed through countless voices and images, shared the remote control, both secretly thinking that the television was killing them, that they should get out more, out into the world against which they could define themselves, and when the remote was in his hands he happened to come across Martin Sheen, of all people, being interviewed on a talk show of the high-minded variety, by a man whose loquacious Southern accent was vaguely familiar.

"Let's watch this for a while," he said.

BARRY LOPEZ

STOLEN HORSES

What we did was wrong, of course, and then it got out of hand, as I suppose such things often do. I knew Ed Hemas from grade school, years ago, before all this. It was his idea. He made it work a few times, and then him and Brett Stallings and Andy Pinticton thought it would work again, and that's how I got into it.

Actually, I don't remember what I thought at the time, twelve years ago. Easy money, and I didn't have any, I guess. I was drifting between high school and whatever when Ed asked and I said, "Sure, I'm in."

He and Brett and Andy had done this twice already, stealing horses and hauling them across the high desert to Burns in the middle of the night, where some guy gave Ed four hundred bucks a head and loaded them on another truck. Thirty head one time, thirty-eight another. Split three ways, cash, of course. You can figure it out.

Andy brought the stock truck down from the Victor Ellen place north of Madras where he worked, tractor-trailer rig. Ed and Brett, they drove Ed's pickup with a two-horse trailer. Ed scouted places around Sisters and down toward Bend where he thought he could get the horses bunched up quiet, away from the house, and then load them in the dark, where all he needed was a little plastic fencing set up, like wings on a chute into the truck. He and Brett wrangled, Andy pushed 'em up the ramp into the trailer.

It took no more than an hour, either time. They did it under a new moon, two in the morning, no one even around maybe on these three-hundred-acre, new-money showplaces. By sunrise they had the truck idling in a stockyard a hundred and fifty miles away in Burns, and Andy had the rig back at the ranch by noon. I don't know what he told his boss about where he'd been with the truck.

The job they asked me about was a place between Sisters and Redmond, sixty head of horses. I knew there were some registered quarters in there, I'd driven by and seen them. Andy wanted a hand with loading. Ed had gotten a deal for five hundred bucks each, so that would be thirty thousand dollars four ways. I should have said no, of course, but it looked good and I didn't care at all about the people who owned the horses.

Here's where my thoughts on this start to run deep. Ed

was selling the horses to a guy who trucked them back to Michigan, back to Ohio. This guy, Ramirez or Sanchez, sold them to people who'd pay a premium for horses that came, as they say, from out West, people just getting into stock market money or lottery money, lawyering or something. Inheritances. Ed thought this Ramirez guy was getting two thousand a head. We were stealing them from the same kind of people in Oregon, people who just got them for show. I know it's not right, but justice is a strange thing, looking at it from my end. My family ranched that central Oregon country for four generations. We took the land from the Indians to start with, but then these people, they took it from us. They came in from Seattle, California, wherever, waving big money around, desperate to get some horses in and look the part. We had to sell. None of us had ever seen money like that.

I know, there's no excuse for theft, not stealing like this, just to get a little extra money and maybe smack some of these people in the face. But anger was a strong feeling, and we all had it. We wanted to fool and rile these people. They could just buy a place they knew nothing about, none of its history or even literally which way the wind blew. And they surely didn't want to be caught around any of us, no more, I guess, than my great grandparents wanted to hang around with the Molala.

No one should have been killed—I didn't even know Ed had a gun until he shot the guy. The other guy, he had no call to run Brett down, it wasn't that sort of a deal. And Ed and Andy, they shouldn't have driven off without me, but you never see these things coming. Maybe you don't want to see it.

I met Ed and Brett that night in a restaurant in Redmond about seven-thirty. We had a few beers and some barbecue and Ed told me about the place. North side of 126, six miles out of Sisters. The horses were in a big pasture along the highway, but there was an access road farther north running parallel, the pasture between them. The only exposure for us, Ed said, was rounding horses up within sight of the highway, but at two in the morning there was no traffic and if there was, a guy could see it a long ways off and get off his horse so he wasn't silhouetted. Ed had drawn us a map—where the road and fences ran, where the house was. It looked simple.

I left my pickup at the restaurant and got into Ed's Ford with him and Brett, their horses saddled in the trailer behind us. Andy was driving in on his own and he was there when we pulled in along the back fence. Ed and Brett unloaded their horses and after Andy and I cut through the fence wire they rode off into the dark. Ed thought it would take him and Brett about thirty minutes to bring the first horses in. We set up the ramp. Andy said we'd load 'em loose. "If they got room enough to fall down," he said, "they got room enough to get up."

The only part of the night I recall without feeling anger or sadness is loading the horses. Andy and I hardly had the fencing up before Brett came along with the first ten or twelve. We had no light, not even a flashlight out, so they weren't easy to see, but I knew horses well enough to know what was there. Well fed, spirited animals, good conformations. A couple of roans and an Appaloosa stood out in that first bunch in the starlight, and a bay with a roached mane. Then Ed brought up a second bunch, about fifteen, mostly dark but a palomino and two paints in there, I remember. Andy and I shooed them up the ramp, which clattered and thundered under their hooves. It was a cool night, still. I could feel the horses on my skin, their body heat swirling around us. I could smell their shit and hear their nostrils fluttering. I felt hard muscle ripple under my hand when I clapped a hip to steer them around. I felt their tails slap my back, and caught a glint in their bared eyes. They jerked their heads and tried to lunge past us, as if they aimed to bolt through the plastic fence. Their feet drummed steady coming toward us on firm ground, feet shot down and pulled up so deftly I heard only the rare click of two hooves. They came up like a big wind in fall cottonwoods.

We waited a good while for the third bunch. I was peering into the night, listening to the jostle and whinny behind me, when I saw the headlights of a vehicle pop up, bucking across the uneven pasture.

Andy just said, "Shit!," slammed the trailer doors shut, and raised the ramp. I guess he meant to drive away, but Ed's truck was in front of him and he couldn't back that trailer through the turns behind him.

For a while I stood there not knowing what had to be done. I could see Ed and Brett, cutting wildly back and forth in front of the vehicle, then I saw the big Suburban hit Brett's horse and him go down. The guy hit his brakes and dust just swallowed everything. Right then I heard a terrific crack—a high-powered rifle—and then two quick light pops from a handgun. Then it was just dust settling in the headlight beams. And silence. The next thing I saw was Ed galloping by. He yanked the horse around in the road, loaded him in the trailer, and him and Andy roared off. It took presence of mind, to load that horse. I was just standing there, and they were gone, running for the highway with the lights off.

Dammit! is all I thought. Damn! Now what? The guy in the Suburban is shot, I guess. Brett's hurt, or worse. I don't want to get caught here. All I could think to do right then was turn the horses back out. I dropped the ramp, opened the doors, and flailed my arms to spook them back to the pasture. I looped a rope quick back and forth in the gap where we'd cut the fence wire and was thinking I should get to Brett when I spotted a vehicle just screaming down the highway, and I ran. I snuck along through the ponderosa and sagebrush till dawn, all the way back to Redmond, where I got my truck.

The police put it together in no time, what with the Ellen truck being there. Andy and Ed had gone on to Burns anyway and got arrested there that night, somebody putting a few things together quickly. Brett had a broken leg, so he went nowhere after he was run over. And Ed, he did kill the guy.

As well as I can understand what happened afterward, Andy and Brett and Ed agreed to leave me out of it. My turning the horses back into the pasture made for a lighter sentence for Brett and Andy, what with the lawyers' bargaining, and they had Ed for murder, anyway.

It never made the papers that I saw, but two years after they sent him up to Pendleton Ed got killed. Andy and Brett did six years and have been out another six now. The murder, there's no statute of limitations on that. One of them, I suppose, could still say something and they'd come after me. But I don't expect it now.

My life got different very soon after that. I moved to Florida, got a job, one I was ashamed of, selling real estate. Got a degree in finance from the University of Miami, and now I run a small business, industrial cleaning company. I have ten employees, meet a payroll, get to a few Dolphins games, and am relatively happy with two kids and all.

I've never understood the economy. I read in the Oregon papers where the guy Ed shot had made a lot of money running a vitamin packaging business on his ranch. My wife works with Cuban refugees teaching English, six dollars an hour. My father, a few years back, took what he got for a quarter-section of our family land along the Deschutes, bought a $185,000 motor home, then lost the rest of it in Las Vegas. He lives in an apartment in Salem now, on what he got for the motor home and some Social Security.

I haven't been on a horse for twelve years, but I remember riding some fine ones. We loaded some that night, and when I see the paints and bays again in my mind I feel the pounding of their feet in my thighs, their body heat on my cheeks. I suppose they all got sold after that, then moved around again, and people made more money off them. Maybe somebody rode one of 'em once in a while. I recall those horses mostly, I believe, because they're not involved in what I'm in. For them there was no place of drifting, trying to decide what would come next. I think about the four of us, young and dumb as fence posts, thinking we'd get ahead. Ahead of what? For three of us it got very bad very fast. Ed, he paid the price, I'd say. Andy and Brett, after something like that, you're almost always going to be behind, the rest of your life. And me, I know there's that price out for me, for what I did. I don't know if I'm ahead or behind. I clean people's offices now. I'm looking for no bill.

JIM SHEPARD

'SCUSE ME, WHILE I KISS THIS GUY

My brother Donnie was acting up again. That was my father's term for it. The police tended to call it assault. My parents had gotten the call from a neighbor in their complex in Florida. They were snowbirds, and summered in Bridgeport. While they were up north, he was down south, in their condo. Every November they passed each other switching homes. Sometimes there'd be an overlap of a few weeks. The idea was to provide him with a rent-free place to stay, and to keep their own exposure to abuse to a minimum. This had been going on for seventeen years.

The neighbor's calls always meant bad news. She'd heard him crashing around and gone up to reason with him. He'd grabbed her arm and thumped her off the wall. She was all right. She'd gone to the emergency room.

My father's MO when down there for those episodes was to throw him out, temporarily: dump him at a fleabag motel with a few hundred dollars. If it was really bad, Donnie went off on foot, and my father got in the car and went looking for him, worried he was going to throw himself under a bus. After a few days they'd meet for breakfast, talk sports, and agree that things couldn't go on this way. Donnie would come back to see a game or grab a meal. Bedtime would roll around and no one would mention the motel. All of this was agonizing for my mother, the old-school Italian: on the one hand, my brother just needed a kick in the ass; on the other, it was my father's call.

They wanted me down there as soon as possible. They called to make small talk and communicate their disappointment that I hadn't gone already. They were the sort of parents that could ask directly only once. I'd said I would go, but I'd said it the way Donnie said he'd do things. What did they think I was going to do down there? I asked. What did they think was going to happen? Was he going to announce that institutionalization was a good idea that hadn't occurred to him?

I called him and floated the idea of visiting. "I got stuff to do," I said, to make things more casual. "But mostly I'd be coming down to see you."

"Sure. C'mon down," he said. "Mr. Science Foundation."

* * *

He was forty-five and hadn't held a job in eight years. When asked, he said he was going to go back to school to study computers. In the meantime he watched TV and made cassette tapes of classical music. He recorded the music off a transistor radio with a condenser mike. He walked to the local Quik Mart for food. He had what my father called episodes, on three- or four-week cycles. When he'd shattered the metal hurricane blinds on the front porch, his neighbors had called the police for the first time.

For the last few years the cops who showed up were on a first-name basis with him. Sometimes he calmed right down and they left him with a warning. A few times he spent the night in jail. He alternated between being proud of and humiliated by what he called his "time in the joint."

His resume, he pointed out to our parents every so often, wasn't like his little brother's. His little brother worked for the Lamont-Doherty Earth Observatory as an oceanologist and sedimentologist. The project proposal on which I was principal investigator broke down its sources of funding by supporting agency: NSF—$259,403; Hudson River Foundation—$140,000; NASA—$1,000,000. When Donnie heard about it, he asked me to send along a copy. The last time I'd visited him, three years or so ago, it had still been on his bedside table. Under the column of award numbers he'd written *Donnie Bilotti—The Olive Grill—$5.45/hr.*

* * *

My mother was famous for her malaprops. My father said she had most of the right letters involved but her tragedy was lining 'em up. She told us that the happiest she'd ever seen Donnie and me was when we were both kids, watching *King Kong vs. Gonzalez.* When asked what her younger son did, she said, "He studies pollution in, you know, seminence." "You know Donnie would do anything for you," she told me, pleading with me to head south and talk him into treatment or an institution. "He'd give you the skin off his back."

They wanted me to try to get him back on Prozac, try to get him to consider using something else, or try to talk him into committing himself. They'd given up on trying to get him to see someone. He never lasted longer than an opening session. I didn't want to go for all sorts of reasons, some of them good. How exactly was my visit going to accomplish anything other than setting him off again? "How would I know?" my mother answered, exasperated. "You're the scientist. You figure it out."

This was my mother's favorite anecdote about us as brothers: I weighed all of three pounds and seven ounces when I was born. It was two months before I came home from the hospital. When I finally did, five-year-old Donnie was even more disappointed. After his first peek into the bassinet, he said, "I can't play with that."

* * *

This was mine: When I was three or four and sucked my thumb, he'd be overcome with something—affection? tenderness? well-being?—and would rush up to me with disconcerting suddenness, cupping both hands around my fist and putting his face nose to nose with mine. I liked it, sensing how much *he* liked it, but I shook him off anyway, with an impatience that even then I knew was halfhearted.

My parents didn't know that Donnie had applied just recently to be a part of the project team at Lamont-Doherty. Our graduate assistant handling the mail brought me his letter. "You might want to see this," she said, like it was a bill from a child pornographer. When she left she shut the door behind her.

It was handwritten and addressed to *Professor Bilotti.* Donnie had written,

> *I would like to apply for work as an assistant in your sedimentology project. I have never worked in that area but I did well in science when I took it. I realize I might be useful only for "grunt" work but I can heft my share. I don't want special treatment but would like to be considered nonetheless. My salary could be completely negotiable.*
>
> *Yours,*
> *Donnie*

I was touched, and panicked. I talked to a couple of colleagues. They looked at me funny. Their feeling was that he could be brought aboard as an intern—I *was* heading the project, after all; it was my call—but that diverting funds for someone with his resume and last name would certainly set off alarms when the accounting was passed along to the NSF or NASA. My coinvestigator cleared his throat before he said "resume."

That whole day I walked around trying to pretend that I was going to help him, that I was going to do something bighearted and reckless.

When I got through to Donnie that night I told him that the good news was that he could come on up as an intern. We couldn't pay him anything, of course, but he could be right there in the thick of things, doing everything I was doing. He was quiet. He was probably looking at that list of funding sources and toting up the numbers.

Why had he written, anyway? I asked. Why hadn't he just called?

"Yeah, I shoulda called," he said.

Say something, I thought. It killed me to hear his voice like that. But I let him do the talking.

"I gotta go," Donnie said. I heard what sounded like an electric can opener.

"So want me to sign you up?" I asked.

"Yeah, I'll think about it," he said. He got off. I called back a few days later and he wasn't answering.

"You don't sound too surprised," my father said when he called a week later to tell me about the blowup.

* * *

He called back at one A.M. that night and made small talk. "I don't know what we're gonna do about your brother," he said, as if that followed.

That was our slogan, year in and year out—it meant *Something's gotta be done. But what can anybody do?* It was our lightning jog through guilt and into absolution. It was a celebration of our good intentions, our announcement that the armless guys were about to roll up their sleeves and get to work.

I booked a four o'clock flight out of LaGuardia for that Wednesday. I called my parents and gave them the good news. That Tuesday I dug up the old photo album my mother had assembled years ago and carried it around my apartment like I was doing prep work for a presentation. My idea of demonstrating brotherly love was sitting around paging through a photo album.

It was one of the more dismal walks down memory lane.

Donnie in his Little League uniform, the *Lordship* in red, his chest so small that the *L* and *P* were hidden, as if he played in the Japanese leagues: *ordshi.* Squinting into the sun and crying, his baseball pants accordioning at his calves where they were tucked into his stirrup socks.

The two of us with me on his lap. He's wearing a narrow, two-toned bow tie. I'm wearing a jumper that looks like a pail. He's worked up a small smile, and I appear stunned. Our cheeks and lips a little suspect, in terms of airbrushed color.

Two baby photos. At *three months,* that expression: things couldn't be worse, but he'd go on, and keep it to himself. Two years later, a professional photo in a paper frame: *Santa and Me.* Santa looking off in one direction, Donnie another, as if sharing an unhappy secret.

Our mother's method in terms of the album's arrangement was a little bit of chronology and a whole lot of whatever was on top of the pile at the time.

What must it have cost her to have assembled this? My father wouldn't have helped, for all sorts of reasons. As far as she was concerned it was a way to remind herself that it hadn't been all misery, and maybe a way to locate some of the mistakes. As far as my father was concerned, it was a way to make yourself miserable all over again, and there was nothing to learn: you didn't flagellate yourself about what you'd been doing during the San Francisco earthquake.

I called Donnie that night to tell him when I was getting in. He had to repeat everything over Hendrix's "Rainy Day, Dream Away" in the background. "Why don't you turn that down?" I told him. "Yeah, I will," he said. The song blared on. He'd discovered Hendrix early, around 1968. My father had called him the Banshee, as in, "Turn that Banshee down." After Donnie got *Are You Experi-*

enced? I went around the house, a long-haired eleven-year-old, singing Hendrix lyrics in a bonding attempt that backfired badly when I ended the chorus from "Purple Haze" with "*'Scuse me, while I kiss this guy.*"

After I called, he called my father to find out whose idea the trip was. My father said he sounded both happy and annoyed. He had no more friends. There was probably no one he'd rather have visit. There was certainly no one he'd feel more betrayed by once he found out what I was doing there.

We spent the year he was fifteen playing five hundred rummy. He'd dropped out of school. He'd taken up weight-lifting and was bulked up. The two of us seemed to have boycotted shampoo. We listened to his record collection nonstop. His collection was fearsome: in 1967 he had John Lee Hooker albums, Little Walter albums, Willie the Lion Smith albums. He took the bus to hole-in-the-wall stores in Bridgeport and dug them up himself. For stretches he shut his door and played album after album and I sat in my room and listened. He could lose his temper at any point. When discussing his situation he was an amazing combination of the world's worst listener and someone who retained everything. A three-year-old remark could set him off. He was our unexploded bomb. At ten I had to work to imagine that sort of power. In my version of him he was a source of crucial wisdom. In his he was a misfit. I thought the lid blew off periodically from the accumulation of too much information. He must've felt like every so often someone just wrenched the handlebars out of his hands and rode him into a ditch.

I flew with the photo album to psych myself into sibling responsibility. The flight landed at eleven forty-five, so I was looking at after midnight before I hit the condo. Midweek was a bad time to be leaving the project to fly to Florida, but there wouldn't be a good time, and I'd been souring on everything anyway: it had begun to feel comic, slogging away to predict the unpredictable. I sat on a packed flight alongside a pretty teenager in the window seat, my mind blank with options. I'd dug up my *Abnormal Psychology* textbook from college and brought it along. I flipped back and forth through it on the tray table every so often, as if boning up. I went back to the photo album. Donnie piloting the strangest riding toy to come out of the fifties: a combination wagon, high chair, and planter, with a lipped tray beneath the steering wheel as if to allow the toddler to eat and drive. Five shots of him on the thing: bleary, happy, happy, vacant, happy.

He'd never gotten over how different we were about school. In classrooms he'd been a fish out of water. I piled up degrees while every year he fell farther behind. Every degree made what he'd be doing more humiliating. Every year he heard about another award. Every year I was off doing something that sounded like it'd be televised on the Nature Channel: seismic reflection profiling or *Alvin* diving. I pioneered a model for the erosion of submarine canyons induced by downslope sediment flows. I went about my life. And never helped him enough, not ever, not once.

I'd tried one night to simplify for my mother the basic question underlying the research to which I was devoting my life. I said, "In terms of the way pollution travels, and slopes fail, how much do we cause, and how much would have happened anyway?" She'd kept her face steady but her eyes had registered that jolt I saw whenever Donnie popped up in her life where she least expected him.

"Nice family," the teenager in the window seat remarked. She had a Louise Brooks haircut and was wearing a man's button-down shirt with the collar turned up. We started talking. She was also going down to visit family, an old aunt. She crinkled her nose.

She'd noticed both the photo album and the textbook. We talked in low airplane voices about Donnie's situation. She had beautiful skin and hair. She looked so taken *care* of. She settled in sideways facing me, impressed by how openly I was willing to talk. I outlined a little of Donnie's suffering, and my parents'.

She had a cousin, she said, who also just freaked out sometimes. After a while she remarked that it was great talking to me. She'd just broken up with a boyfriend, also eighteen, and he'd never been able to talk like this.

I'd used Donnie this way before. We used what we had, I guessed.

I opened the album to Donnie as a five-year-old ring-bearer at his aunt's wedding. He sported an ivory jacket and a black bow tie as narrow as a clothespin. His expression was blank, but the little girl he'd been partnered with was looking at him with real apprehension.

The teenager's name was Catherine. I liked her. "Oh, he was cute," Catherine said, sad for his sake. I nodded. She looked at pictures of him as a teenager and decided that he was hot. I told her I'd set her up, and it embarrassed her. She chuckled at an identification card he'd filled out in fourth grade: name and address and teacher and the last five digits of his phone number, and under that, painstakingly printed in block letters, IN CASE OF AN ACCIDENT, CALL A PRIEST.

She was doing a thesis in Bio but had come really close to majoring in Geology. Toward the end of the flight she said she didn't know if I did this—saw younger people—but—She got embarrassed again. She didn't know anybody down here, she added. She tore a page out of her address book and wrote her number on it. I thanked her and wrote Donnie's number in her book. Then she went back to her novel, mortified and excited. On the way out of the plane, I told her it was great talking to her and that I'd call. She said the perfect thing: she said, I hope you will, just that simply.

He wasn't at the gate. *That figures,* I thought. I sounded like my father. Catherine made her way past me and smiled but she looked back twice to try and see the brother. After she disappeared I caught sight of him keeping an eye out for me three gates down, as if he hadn't wanted to seem too eager. It looked like he'd been at the weights again. His shoulders were getting a real Schwarzenegger spread to them. When I said hello he couldn't contain his smile. He looked away and stuck out a hand. "How ya doin'," he said. His handshakes were always feeble, like he'd decided not to break your hand and had overcompensated the other way.

He asked about the flight. He asked about our parents. On the way back from the airport we talked sports. His driving hadn't improved, especially the staying-between-the-lines part. He was going to go a few days and then he was going to bring up the project team. We both knew how this was going to work.

We also both knew that his application to be part of it hadn't been *only* crazy. Forty years of voluntary and involuntary outsider status had made him savvy about institutional logic and inflexibility. He'd helped me out before. In the middle of a miserable first semester my senior year we'd had a phone conversation that strayed off movies and sports long enough for me to let him in on my latest insurmountable problem: organizing a team of peers who'd be helping out on my senior thesis. There were personalities I couldn't handle, a problem I found paralyzing, and my advisor was uninteresting. I had no idea how to proceed, other than lying awake all night. Donnie's suggestion had been to make the asshole the boss. Feed him what I wanted and congratulate him on having thought of it. It sounded great, except what about the other kids? What would they think about my having promoted the asshole? "And you care about that why, exactly?" Donnie had said. It had worked out perfectly. The asshole took the bait and the thesis won a college-wide award, and greased my way into the graduate school of my dreams. Maybe I would have gotten in anyway. I'll never know. I bought Donnie a two-volume history of baseball. I told my parents how much I owed him, but they didn't get it, and I didn't work to make sure they did.

At the condo my bag fell open and the photo album and textbook almost spilled out. That would've been nice, I thought. He told me I'd be sleeping in our parents' room. A while ago he'd commandeered what they had hoped would be the guest room. On the way to my room I peeked into his. His desktop was a skyline of audiocassettes. A pile performed a slow spill down the bed he wasn't using. They were labeled in pencil, so lightly you had to hold them to your eye to read them. He taped everything in the order he heard it, so a label would read *Bach/ST. MATTHEW's P—Interview w/Paul Schrader—Bonanza theme.* It occurred to me that everything he'd ever done had been about getting rid of dead time, time to think.

On the floor in a corner there was half a tuna sandwich on a plastic plate. His clothes were in an open suitcase on the dresser. For the last twenty years he'd kept them in the suitcase to remind himself that he was only staying anywhere a day or two. One Christmas they bought him a duffel, but he preferred the suitcase.

It served as a bookend for a line of library books: Ryan and McHugh's *Sedimentology,* Cowles's *Principles of Geology,* and Tarr and Heinemann's *Geologic Data Analysis.* The tops were bookmarked like stegosaurs.

"I been doin' some reading," he said.

"I see that," I said. There was a pause. I suggested a beer.

My mother complained to him once when he was shooting himself in the foot about something or other that he'd only make himself miserable, and he broke a table lamp in half the way movie guys break the necks off beer bottles and screamed at her, "You think I don't *know* what I'm doing? How stupid do you think I am?"

We watched TV. He kept the shades pulled. I thought about Catherine. I told him that I had some meetings I might have to go to in the next few days. He talked about his most recent tapes, and what great radio stations there were in south Florida. Two days went by like that. We might as well have been in Manitoba. On the third day we went out for breakfast and I got to see the sun.

While he was in the men's room I called her. She suggested brunch. When we got back to the condo I told Donnie I had a meeting. "When?" he said. "Now," I said. He shrugged and got out of the car.

She was already in a booth when I got there. She'd hung her sunglasses on the front of her Black Dog tank top.

She asked how things were going. She asked when I'd last visited. She blanched at the answer. "You haven't visited him in *three years*?" she said.

"Nope," I said.

I shook my head back and forth. A waitress nodded that she'd be over soon. "I'm ready for you to go on," Catherine said.

"It doesn't help that much when I do visit," I said. "You know."

She gave that some thought. "Is he dangerous?" she said.

"Not really," I said.

She looked dissatisfied. I was disappointing her. I told her my thumb-sucking anecdote. I thought it was sweet.

"*That's* your favorite anecdote?" she said.

I nodded, looking down at the table. "So tell me more about the guy you just broke up with," I finally said. We talked about him until it was time for the check. She warmed up a little to that.

"I'm sure I'm an even worse brother than I'm coming across," I told her when we were saying good-bye.

"Not necessarily," she said.

When I got back Donnie was in his room and the door was open. The music was going. I sat on the floor. A Tom Lehrer concert was sutured onto a John Williams retrospective. When it came time to flip the tape he said, "Someone named Catherine called right before you got back."

I told him she must've been trying to set up another meeting.

"She likes meetings," he said. I agreed.

He suggested I call her back. I told him I would. He seemed to be waiting, so finally I did. She told me she just wanted to say she was sorry she'd seemed so hard on me. I tried to keep my responses neutral enough to sound professional. She said she'd been thinking about me. She asked how old I was. We worked out a meeting at a bar for nine that night.

When I got off I asked Donnie if that was all right with him. "What do I care?" he said.

He watched me the rest of the day. We listened to more music. I knew we needed to have some sort of meaningful conversation before I went off again. He was already hurt that I'd gotten so bored in two days. I hated that I'd waited so long and hated having to say anything at all. I'd worsened an already bad situation to flirt with an eighteen-year-old. It enraged me that he needed me so much. Who in their right mind needed me?

We had dinner late. We were just sitting there waiting for nine o'clock. "You still taking that stuff?" I finally said.

"I been reading about sedimentology," he said. "Lotta what I been reading's real interesting."

"A lot of it is," I said. "It's a pretty amazing field. So you been off the Prozac, more or less?"

"Everybody has ideas about what I need," Donnie said. "I'm supposed to listen to everyone but me."

"It's not like anybody's so sure about anything," I said.

"So you thought any more about that thing? That letter I sent?" he asked.

"Yeah. Sure," I said.

Off in his room a cassette tape was still going. Someone was being interviewed and was pausing to think through a question. The kitchen clock said eight thirty-five, but it was a little fast.

"It's not like I need a lot of money," Donnie said.

"No," I said.

"But, you know, I'm not taking charity here," he said.

"No," I said.

"So you don't need me?" he said.

"It's not that we don't need you," I said.

"You don't need me, you don't need me," he said. He shrugged. We listened to the tape.

"I hear you had some excitement down here," I said. He

ignored me. "I think you should, you know, think about taking that stuff again," I said.

" 'That stuff'?" he asked. He'd lowered his voice.

He got up and left the room. I heard the tape change. When he came back he didn't bother to identify what was coming next. I had the same impulse my father always had: calm him down, don't push it any more.

"They think you should try something else if that doesn't work," I said. *They* was code for our parents.

He hadn't sat back down yet. He was just standing near the kitchen table. He made a bridge on his forehead with his thumb and middle finger. "I just need, you know, something to occupy myself. I gotta get *occupied,*" he said.

He stuck out his lower lip and mugged: Poor Sad Me.

I thought, *I'll hire him out of my own pocket. Our parents can chip in. He'll never find out.* "Maybe we could put you on salary," I said.

"Doing *what*?" he snarled. When his anger finally cut loose it was always a jolt, no matter how long you'd been expecting it.

"I don't know," I said. I cast around for something. "Seismic reflection data. Collecting and interpreting."

He snorted. That was his little brother, for you: lying, lying, lying.

"There's a lot a things you could do," I finally said.

"Do you have the first fucking idea what you're talking about?" he asked. "The slightest idea?"

"C'mon," I said.

"Do you have *any idea* how fucked up I am? Do you?"

It was one of those questions that over the years I'd learned not to answer.

"I should be insti*tu*tionalized," he said. "I should be *taken* the fuck out of circulation."

We sat there, not knowing what to do next.

"Well, maybe you should," I said.

He snorted again.

"No," I said. "You know. Have you ever looked into that?"

He pursed his mouth. I cleared my throat.

"Let me ask you something," Donnie said. "You have the balls to come down here and say that to me?"

"Donnie," I said.

"You have the balls to fly down here with your—Abnormal Psychology textbook and say that to me?"

He took a step closer and then sat in the chair next to mine. We were looking at each other. His expression suggested that every so often everything that enraged him coalesced right in front of him, and at such moments he had to mull over whether or not to vent himself on the universe. I tried not to move.

This was what I was willing to do for him, I realized. Not integrate him into my life but let him hurt me, seriously, for the first time. That was the breakthrough I preferred. I imagined my parents' faces afterward, in the hospital. And I knew what I deserved.

The phone rang. He didn't get up. After five rings I asked if he wanted me to get it. I needed to clear my throat. He didn't answer. It kept ringing and then it stopped.

It wasn't that I never helped him. It was that I always helped him on my own terms.

He spread his fingers and looked at the back of his hand. He indicated the clock. "Go to your meeting," he said.

"I don't have to," I said. I kept having to clear my throat. "I'll call."

We sat there while he went over the humiliating parts of all this in his head again.

He said, "All those fucking *years* you *ignore* me and then I finally ask for something and you have the balls to come down here and say that to me?" No one on earth, anywhere, had the capacity for humiliation that Donnie did.

"C'mon," I said.

"No, this is good advice," he said. "Instead of coming up and getting a job with you like a human being I should just hide myself the fuck away down here and never see anybody again."

"I'm going out," I said, standing up. I had just enough courage for that.

"Yeah, you go out," Donnie said. "Go see Catherine. Hit the nightclubs. Disco down."

I found the car keys and left. By the time I got to the car it sounded like a Cossack raid back up in the apartment. Something big went over and there was splintering and shattering after that. I took the stairs two at a time. I pounded on the door but he wouldn't unlock it. I remembered the downstairs neighbor and the spare key and ran back down to her door. She was out in the hall already, with her neighbors. She was the woman he'd assaulted. I asked for the key. We were awkward. She got it for me and I ran back upstairs.

The living room furniture was in the middle of the room. He'd taken a bat to it. The curio cabinet had turned out to be laminate and not real wood.

He was in one of the bedrooms, breaking things. I called for him as I went down the hall.

Had we ever been each other's playmates? Once after he'd thrown me over an end table our father had intervened and they'd grappled in a scary two-step while I'd picked myself out of the rubble. I'd tried to join in, not wanting to be left out, thinking this was what we did best.

My parents' room was closer. It was untouched. I turned the corner to his and books and furniture and debris seemed to be in free play in terms of gravity, and a metal desk lamp flew end over end into the bridge of my nose. The cartilege made a walnut-shell sound. I fell, holding my face. My eyes teared. From along the wall Donnie came rushing, crying himself, his face nose to nose and his hands coming up around mine, his body overcome with something. I hit the wall with my back and slid to the floor. He had me by both hands and was holding me still for something. I welcomed it all, whatever it was. Either because of all I'd done or all I hadn't or both, my brother was leading me through, as he had before, what we meant by family feeling.

BRIDGET
ROHAN
GARRITY

THE HOLY BOYS

Ma sits beside me in the front seat, and the car reeks of mothballs from my suit. Ma's lost weight, and her old black dress coat comes up around her face like she's peering out a hole. Snowbanks line Dot Street, ruined by soot now, but not melting. Murphy's said that even though the ground is still frozen they'll dig Pauly his grave, force the ground open with a jackhammer if they have to. I hear my brother's voice *Emmie, it's Pauly here* and think how even his grave won't take him. But I stop myself, *Hell no, Pauly, you're not taking me with you,* and reach for my cigarettes.

"Off with the lead shoe already," Ma says. "We can't afford any more funerals in this family." She has a wad of Kleenex in her hands, but so far she's used it only to blot her lips.

I sigh, ease up on the pedal. My suit coat is on me like a straitjacket, and I round out my shoulders a couple of times to loosen it.

"I want you to keep that suit coat buttoned at the wake."

"It's too damned tight."

"You had plenty of time to buy yourself a new one. A thirty-one-year-old boy should be able to buy himself a suit."

Our Chevy rattles up the Heights, past Flynn's On Tap and old guys smoking on doorsteps. Past empty lots. When I was a kid, there were always rumors that something was coming to fill these lots: *A McDonald's is coming. A new movie theater is coming. A community center is coming.* None of those things ever came. I motion to a lot as we go past. "Ma. In that lot over there: The Paul Patrick O'Toole Community Skating Arena. What do you think?"

She frowns. "What do you mean what do I think? I don't know what the hell you're talking about."

"In Pauly's memory. A rink. Maybe have some fund-raisers. Car washes, bake sales, like that."

She turns her face to the window. "If we're going to have any fund-raisers, it'll be to pay off this funeral. A hockey rink? For God's sake. Just the casket is a thousand dollars. A thousand dollars. For a *casket.* For that much it oughta resurrect him."

"Jesus, Ma."

"The open house, the flowers, the headstone . . ." She

shakes her head. "Costs more to be dead than alive anymore. When I was a girl, we buried my mother in a pine box. And as far as I know, it did just what it was supposed to do. But Murphy says, 'Send him home like a prince, I'll give you a rate.' Yeah, he gave us a rate all right. What a crock. It was the same thing when your father died. We should've gone somewhere else. Your father wasn't even friends with him at the VFW, that's what burns me—"

"Ma, take a breath."

"We've got to get this car fixed before it breaks down for good and all. And that damned leak in the basement." She sighs. "Like my father always said—" She crosses herself.

Same old shit. Like she's reading from a script. "It takes a lot of money to be poor."

"Oh, you know that so well, do you? Well, you don't know it as well as you're going to know it, believe me. I pray to God every day you never know money trouble like I've known money trouble."

Out on the sidewalk a kid shoves a fistful of snow down another kid's jacket. "Just an idea, Ma."

"Yeah, well, ideas are your biggest problem. Always stuck inside your head. Having dreams is nice, but you got to wake up now and again." She stops suddenly, realizes she's going too hard on me, and the excitement in her face stills. She pulls down the visor and looks in its mirror, dabs her Kleenex at lipstick that's bled into the wrinkles around her mouth. "But I know your heart is in the right place.

You were always a good boy to your brother." Without looking at me, she reaches for my hand, but my hand is on the wheel, so she pats the dash.

I glance at her. Her mouth is tense, but her eyes are dull and dry, and I look away. They found Pauly in an alley off Downtown Crossing, shot in the head. Ma said she couldn't take anymore, so I've been doing the talking with the cops. When I went to ID him, I stood there for a long time, waiting to feel something. The back of his head was gone, but the scar above his eyebrow was still there, from the State Championship against Worcester in '81, when his mask slipped up and the puck hit him in the face. The only things they had of his were his wheelchair and his wallet, empty but for one of those posed prom photos of him and Moira, a fake palm tree hanging over them. I looked hard at that photo. Pauly hadn't looked that way in a long time, not even in my mind: chin lifted, eyes fighting off a laugh. The Pauly in my mind had hard eyes and a mean set to his jaw. The kid in the photo looked more like me than him, and I can't get that out of my head.

"When did your brother say he'd be there?"

"He didn't."

"I don't want you two picking at each other today either. He's driving all night from South Carolina and I don't want trouble."

"I'm not gonna say a word."

"Did you bring the trophies?"

"Yeah, I brought the trophies."

She looks at me. "What's your problem?"

"Nothing. I brought them, okay?"

She sits there scowling for a minute. Then she says, "I don't see anything wrong with wanting people to remember the old Pauly. The real Pauly. I don't want people remembering my son as a bum. My son was not a bum."

"Ma, I didn't say anything. I brought them, okay?"

She sighs again and a darkness moves over her face. The sidewalks are empty but for a few old people with canes, inching their way to noon mass at St. Augustine's, "cramming for finals," as Ma would say. It's only the old people who go to church anymore. Ma's always saying, "The town ain't what it used to be," but I've been hearing that for as long as I can remember. Sometimes I imagine myself in Florida or out West, maybe opening a pro shop somewhere or managing a team.

"I just thank God your father isn't here to see this," Ma says. "It would have killed him. He wouldn't have survived it. But now they're together again. We just have to concentrate on finding who did this to our Pauly, and then somehow make peace with it. That's what Pauly would've wanted."

I bear down on the pedal as we near the crest of the hill and St. Augustine's Cemetery, chalky tombstones twisted in the snow. I remember me and Pauly running around with toy guns, hiding behind the monuments. Now they keep the gates locked. No matter where I hid, Pauly always found me, came up behind me and put the plastic barrel to my head. *Bang Bang, Emmie. You're dead.*

* * *

The room fills, first with people, then with smoke. The Cookes, the O'Connells, Father Frank, old hockey buddies of Pauly's, City Councilor Kelly, neighbors and relatives and people I've never met who were fans of Pauly's on the ice. Murphy is walking around like he's looking for votes, patting people on the back, offering cigars. The place itself makes me feel like hell—faded red carpet, gaudy glass light fixtures, the smell of old smoke everywhere. When we came here for Dad's funeral, Pauly said it looked like a Turkish whorehouse and Ma threatened to slap him.

At the back of the room, Jimmy sits brooding in a folding chair. He's seven years younger than I am, always the baby to me and Pauly, only five when Dad died. Still a kid when Pauly lost his legs and all the trouble started. In his face you can see what those years took from him. He joined up with the marines right after high school, damn near showed up at Lejeune in his cap and gown. Beside him Angela plays with the baby. She's Jimmy's high school sweetheart, from the North End. Behind her back Ma calls her "Jimmy's Guinea."

Ma's still fiddling with the trophy display, arranging ribbons and newspaper clippings on a card table Murphy brought up from the basement. This morning when I was grabbing awards off Pauly's shelves, I took a good look at the MVP All-State trophy, remembered the night he won it. When they announced his name, Ma had put her hands over her face to hide her crying, and that night I'd lain in bed sleepless, replaying the look on her face. Pauly wrapped up the trophy and gave it to me for my fifteenth birthday. When he saw I was on the verge of bawling, he started laughing and put me in a headlock. *God knows you'd never earn one of your own, you lazy little shit.* But after the accident, Ma took it off my shelf and put it back on Pauly's side. She never said anything about it; I just remember that one day I looked up and it was gone. When I saw it on Pauly's shelf, I put it back on mine. A couple of days later, there it was on his side again. She used to come in and dust his trophies, but somewhere along the line she stopped doing that. Now the MVP trophy is the centerpiece of the display she's arranged. There are streaks of dust from it on her skirt.

Guests mingle, kneel at the casket. Mrs. Griffin is here from St. Monica's, playing the organ like an ass she's trying to kick. The Sullivans come in, Sully clean-shaven and holding Aunt Mary by the elbow. I'll always think of Sully as he was at ten, freckle-faced, foul-mouthed. He nods to me with a seriousness that makes me grin. Big man of the house.

After a while Ma comes up to me and says I should be near the casket to receive people. She goes back to her little display, greeting people as they come in. The casket is closed, covered with flowers. As I take my place beside it, it occurs to me Ma has never seen him dead. I try to imagine how she would have reacted if she'd seen him the way I did, but I can't conjure her expression.

The line starts moving, grievers coming one after the other, until all the faces and voices become a single echo.

Our prayers are with you. We'll bring a dish by. Do they have any leads? So many sick, sick people out there. I remember when you and Pauly used to come around with penny candy and sell them for a quarter each. The town hasn't had a goalie since who comes close. He always seemed to blame himself for what happened to the Fagan girl. Accidents happen, it's not always someone's fault. You were always a fine brother to him, but that's the kind of people you come from.

I look out at the crowd. All the people from our childhood. Teachers, coaches. Grown-up faces of the kids we used to run with—Feeney, White, Tommy Harrington. After the accident, everyone was there for him, visitors all the time, kids coming by. It kept him going for a while. He thought about still going to college, maybe getting a degree in sports administration. U. Mass. said they'd make good on their offer, even if he couldn't play. I don't know what happened to all that.

I keep greeting people, but I can't shut out Ma's voice beside me. She keeps saying the same things to people, until I wonder if maybe she's delirious. "We'll find who did this and they'll pay. We didn't know what more to do but love him." But the more I watch her, the more I know she's not delirious at all. There's too much trying in her face.

Mrs. Gannon approaches Ma, all sad-sack. I want to remind the old bitch she's called the cops on Pauly about ten times over the last few years. Every time she saw him coming she got on the phone. Now she gives Ma a hug.

"My prayers are with you, Eily. Let me know what I can do."

"Thank you, Betty," Ma says. "What could we do? We didn't know what more to do but love him. But at least now he's at peace."

"He's where he belongs, Eily."

I see Pauly in his chair in the middle of the street, looking up at our house like a kid.

I don't allow drugs in this house. I've told him time and time again.

Ma, for Christ's sake, it's cold out there. Just for tonight.

I can't have that in my house. I can't have the police here one more time. Now go tell him another night.

Ma, come on. I can't do that.

How much do I have to take? Tell me.

I'm shocked to see the Fagans coming toward me. Mrs. Fagan reaches for me weakly. She's tiny like Moira was, and as we hug I have the stupid notion I might hurt her. Mr. Fagan stands slightly behind her, somber-faced and silent.

"Thanks so much for coming," I say to them. "It would have meant a lot to Pauly." And it would have. He couldn't go to Moira's funeral because he was still in the hospital, so me and Ma went for him. Mrs. Fagan turned her back on Ma in the receiving line, but now she stands in front of me, weeping. When I turn to Mr. Fagan, he looks past me, into the crowd.

Mrs. Fagan moves to the casket and kneels, drops her head in prayer. It hurts to look at her, but I don't know it's sadness I feel. I close my eyes and press my fingers into them for a second. *I'm sorry, Pauly. Not tonight.*

Not tonight? Not tonight? What the hell does that mean, "not tonight"? Emmie, what the Christ? It's Pauly here.

Someone is in front of me, shaking my hand. "Thank you so much," I say. "It's good of you to come." The day I ID'd him, I asked the medical examiner if there was any chance he did it to himself. She said not much of one, judging from the wound. She said a couple of other "homeless individuals" had been brought in recently. I told her Pauly had a home.

I leave my place near the casket, sort of nodding in apology to no one in particular. "Ma," I whisper to her as I move past, "I'm gonna get some air." I don't wait for her to answer.

On my way through the crowd, I feel a firm grip on my shoulder, and I'm relieved to see it's Father Frank. He's a large man with a jowl-hung face and a sad, slow voice. I've known him for as long as I can remember. Father Frank is from the neighborhood, went to grade school and high school with my dad.

He shakes my hand solemnly. "Well, now, that's a suit, isn't it," he says.

"Maybe you remember it from my First Communion," I say, showing him how I can barely move my arms.

Father laughs. Then he takes my arm, lowers his voice. "You've been such a support to your mother, Emmet. You've been a pillar of strength for the whole family." His tone disappoints me. He's in prime funeral mode; I could be anybody. "I just want you to know what a fine son you've been. You make her very proud."

"I think you should go to her for a second opinion."

He laughs. "No, no, she told me herself. She doesn't know what she'd do without you. You're her saving grace."

"I'm working on building a rink. As a tribute to Pauly."

"You don't say? That's marvelous."

"Yeah, I'm pulling together donations."

"Well, let me know what I can do." He glances at the trophy display and grins. "Oh, but I remember you two so well as boys. I'll never forget the day the doorbell rang and there on the stoop were you two—'Father, we'd like to be your holy boys.' Holy boys!" His old eyes water with laughter. "And from then on, every Sunday there were the two of you, rolling around in your cassocks, wrestling for the bells."

I can't help but laugh. "Yeah, and he always got 'em. Except that time my birthday fell on a Sunday and he forfeited them to me." We used to sneak wine too. I consider telling him but decide against it.

"Worst enemies. And best friends, you two."

"Beat me at everything. Especially on the ice."

"He was a regular song-and-dance man on the ice, wasn't he? But everyone's strength takes a turn, and you were there for him. In his victories and defeats."

I'm relieved to feel Ma tugging at my arm. She and Father embrace. "We couldn't give him what he needed, Father. But I did the best I could."

"I know you did, Eily," he whispers. "And God knows."

" 'Scuse us, Father." She pulls me to the window, and points out. "What the hell is all that?" she whispers. Out at the curb there's a group of what appear to be homeless guys, smoking and talking among themselves. Several cabs are parked along the street too, the drivers in a huddle. "And is that your brother out there? Go get that boy and tell him to get his ass in here."

The air outside has a bite and I'm glad to feel it. Jimmy is leaned up against a car, shivering and smoking. "What's all this?" I ask. He hands me his pack.

"Pauly's fan club, looks like."

I feel the homeless guys and the cabbies eyeing me. The cabbies looked out for Pauly, gave him rides back to the neighborhood now and again. I hear myself yelling, "Hey, fellas, feel free to go on in and pay respects if you want." They look back at me like I've just told them to fuck off.

"Ma'd love that," Jimmy says.

"I don't know. They came all the way over. And it's damn cold out here." I rub my neck. "How's the South treating you?"

"Good, good."

"Think I'd like it down there?"

He shrugs. "Come down and see for yourself."

"Yeah, I will." I dig my heel into a patch of ice. "Not

right now though. Ma needs a man around. It's not safe for her to be in that house alone."

He laughs. "Em, you're the only man of the house I know who sleeps under a poster of Bobby Orr."

I remind myself not to get into it with him. I fix my eyes on Murphy's sign. Green and gold. *A STRANGER IS JUST A FRIEND WE'VE YET TO MEET.* We stand in silence for a while, watching the homeless guys and cabbies talk and laugh.

"How's things at Gillette?"

I shrug and take a drag. "It's a job."

"You planning on staying there for a while?"

I nod. "Good benefits. Health, dental, the whole nine. I've been saving a little too."

"Good for you."

Pauly's friends break out in laughter. One of the street guys, the ring leader it seems like, is telling a story, and I can tell that it's about Pauly. At one point he sort of mimes Pauly operating his chair, which he whipped around like some kind of lethal carnival ride. They're all laughing and laughing, and I try and hear, but I can't piece it together.

"Any more information," Jimmy asks.

"Not to speak of," I say. "Not a hell of a lot to go on. No gun, no witnesses. They keep telling us not to hold our breath."

"Pauly own a gun?"

I look at him. "No. Not that I knew of anyway." When he doesn't say anything, I add, "I guess a couple of other guys like Pauly got it, too. They think it might be some kind of gang initiation or some such shit."

He drops his head. "Jesus."

"Listen," I say to him finally, "what would you say about building a rink for Pauly? For the kids. You still know some people. We could go to the Kiwanis, the Knights, maybe have a telethon."

His scowl breaks with laughter. "A telethon? Jesus Christ, Em."

"Hey, asshole, it's possible. Think about it."

He flings his butt into the snow and crosses his arms. "Don't you ever wonder, Em? What the hell would you ever have done with yourself if Pauly hadn't fucked himself up?" He looks at me. "Think about it."

"Just shut your mouth, all right?"

"She wears you like a crutch, Em."

I shake my head and begin walking back to the funeral home. Ice cracks under my dress shoes. I feel the bums' and cabbies' eyes fixed on me again, and it occurs to me they see Pauly in my face. I keep my head down. Without turning around I tell Jimmy that the service is about to start and that Ma wants him in there.

Father Frank has on his purple vestments and is standing by the casket with his head bowed and his palms raised and open. Ma's at the front, gesturing to me to take the seat beside her, but I wave her off as if it's too crowded, and take a spot at the back of the room.

"Lord, those who die still live in your presence. And your saints rejoice in complete happiness. Listen to our prayers for Paul Patrick O'Toole, your son, who has passed from the light of this world, and bring him to the joy of eternal radiance. We ask this in the name of your son, Jesus Christ."

The crowd responds: *Forever and ever. Amen.*

Suddenly there's a chorus of honks, and when I look out the window I see the cabbies, lying on their horns and laughing. Then the bums start up: *Pauly! Pauly! Pauly!* Marching around like they're in a parade, laughing their asses off. I grin. I know he would have loved it. Pauly loved hoopla. Around me the mourners turn to each other, some of them chuckling, others not knowing what to do. I see Sully with his hand over his mouth, trying not to laugh. Ma looks up, stunned. Her eyes are searching for me, but I turn back to the window.

Father stops for a moment and smiles, then continues, yelling above the chants. "Out of lament for the suffering of Paul Patrick, O Lord, we conduct today's rosary in honor of the Five Sorrowful Mysteries of your son, Jesus Christ. We begin with the mystery of Christ's agony in the garden as he awaited betrayal. Hail Mary, full of grace . . ."

I watch Ma in the front row. Her hands are manacled in a rosary. For years after the accident, I'd lie in bed hearing her mumbling the rosary for him beyond the bedroom wall. When he was still at home, Pauly slept downstairs on the couch—he wouldn't let anyone carry him upstairs—and sometimes I'd go over and get in his empty bed. We'd shared that room our entire lives, and every night we lay talking, staring up at the cracks in the ceiling. Going over Pauly's games play by play. Making plans. I was going to be his agent when he went pro, and when he retired we'd build a rink, the O'Toole Arena. It seems stupid to me now, but then I believed.

Things must have been okay for a while, and as I stand there listening to Father I try to remember what happened, where things got screwed up, but only certain images come to me. Walking into the kitchen and finding Ma in her nightgown, crying, sopping up piss with a kitchen sponge. Bandaging his arms where he'd made cuts on himself. And the screaming. Even now I can hear him, and Ma crying and begging, the cops pounding on the door.

Ma's head is bent, her expression strained. And it occurs to me as I watch her that she hasn't yet knelt at Pauly's casket.

After the liturgy a group of Pauly's friends from the streets wander in. They seem nervous and awkward, and I go over to them and shake their hands. The cold comes off them like breath. Their chapped faces remind me of the street Pauly, and I want to say something or do something for them. I motion toward the trophy display and they go to it, picking up the metals and ribbons, grinning and passing them back and forth. Ma looks up from her rosary, and our eyes lock for a second.

From behind me I hear a whisper. "Want some air?" Sully. His code words for a beer.

"God, yeah." I head toward Ma to let her know, but

when I approach her, she's talking to someone, saying the same shit, and I turn and follow Sully out the door.

We stop at Store 24 so Sully can buy some chances. When we were kids, the store was Tippy's Five and Dime. I'd go up to the counter and buy something to distract old Tippy while Pauly stuffed his pockets with penny candy. Now I stand outside smoking, squinting into the gray light.

"Gimme a coin," Sully says when he comes out. He's got an Easy Street ticket, a five-dollar ticket. "I feel lucky today," he says. He begins to scratch. "I win, I'll buy you anything you want. You and me'll take a trip down to Daytona. No! The Bahamas. A cruise to the Bahamas."

"Let's build a rink," I say. "As a tribute to Pauly."

He stops scratching, looks at me. "The rink. That's exactly what we're supposed to do." Sully gets dramatic at times; now his expression is far off, as if he's already won. "We'll build a rink for Pauly." He starts to scratch again. "And with the money that's left, I'll take a cruise to the Bahamas."

I grin and shake my head. "Let's get up the street already. I only have time for one."

Sully scratches all the boxes but one; then he stops. "For Pauly," he says, and crosses himself. He scratches the last box, then crumples it, hurls it like a stone. "Son of a bitch."

We start heading up the street. I don't have a coat on, and the wind cuts through my suit. I curl my hands under my arms. Sully keeps his arms stiff at his sides, defying the cold. Our dress shoes click on the pavement.

Flynn's is empty but for a couple of old guys nursing the midmorning shakes. When we come in, their eyes are small, almost fearful in the light that pierces the room.

Sully nods to them, then says, "Today's are on me," and pulls out his wallet. He orders a couple and lights up.

I grab a cigarette and look up at the TV. CNN—civilians being carried away in bloody sheets. Old women keening over bodies. The two old guys at the end of the bar blink drowsily up at the pictures, tap their butts against ashtrays. I think of Dad down at the VFW, me and Pauly going in there to pester him for a couple of bucks. He always drank a shot with his beer, and he'd give us a sip from both. *Quiet about it. What your mother doesn't know won't hurt her.*

"Oh, man." He exhales. "That's the weirdest fucking wake I ever been to. All those fucking street rats milling around."

"Least he had friends out there."

"Friends?" he says. "He had friends in the neighborhood if he would have stuck around. Look at all the people there today. Those are his friends. Everybody loved Pauly."

I keep my mouth shut. Jackie sets our beers down. "On the house," he says. "To Pauly."

I shake his hand. "Thanks, Jackie." I nudge Sully. "Your kind of tab."

We drink and smoke without talking for a while. Being

with Sully's like being alone most the time, and though sometimes it puts me in a mood, today I'm glad for it. We just sit and drink until one of the old guys begins hacking, and he keeps it up until I think his guts are going to come out his mouth. He keeps his eyes fixed on me, his face purple. I turn the other way. "Jesus."

"What the Christ," Sully hisses, and turns to the old man. "Hey, Bill, you okay over there? No dropping while I'm setting here enjoying one, okay?" The old guy nods. Jackie hands him a napkin without taking his eyes off the TV.

We drink some more—a couple of beers, a couple of shots. Jackie keeps setting them down in front of us. Then I say to him, "Hey, Jackie, we're putting together a rink in the neighborhood in Pauly's honor. How about setting out a cup for donations?"

He gets a beer glass and sets it on the bar. Then he picks it up and sets it down in front of the old guys. They pull out their scrappy wallets, throw in a few bucks each, and nod toward me. Then Jackie picks up the glass and sets it in front of us.

"Awesome, a rink for Pauly," Sully says. He sticks the tip of his finger into his shot glass and licks. Then he dumps the money out of the glass onto the bar and counts it. "Six bucks," he says. "Hey, it's a start."

"Thanks, Sully." But looking at him and the beer glass in front of me hits me with something, and I suck in a breath and wait for it to pass. I can hear Pauly laughing. *Hey, you got a doorknob's worth there.*

After a while Sully asks, "Boston PD moving on the case at all?"

I shrug and blow a line of smoke in the air. "They're talking to people. It's hard when it's a situation like Pauly's. Street code and all that. No one's talking."

Sully burps, then covers his mouth with a fist. He waves the comment away. "Don't let them give you that shit. You can bet your ass if it was a Kennedy or somebody, they'd find who did it."

"They've been all right."

Looking into the mirror behind the bar, Sully says, "My heart goes out to your ma. Your ma's a living saint, Toolie, I've always said so."

I say nothing, take another gulp.

" 'Member when Pauly used to hang out down by the courts? Playing coach and all that? One day I walked past the court at Old Colony, and there he was, sitting under the hoop in his chair, just waiting for kids to show up." Sully thinks for a minute, then shakes his head and laughs. "And he was a tough fucker too. All these little kids heading down there for a few laughs, and here's this bastard in a wheelchair on the sidelines, 'Defense, you little shit, defense!' "

We both laugh. Ma used to make me go find him and bring him a lunch.

"What happened with all that," Sully asks. "Why didn't he stick with it? I bet they could have taken him on at the high school. As an assistant coach or something."

"I don't know. I don't know what happened."

Sully frowns into his empty shot glass. "They never thought . . . I mean, it was never possible that he—" Then he shakes his head and wipes his mouth with the back of his hand.

"What?"

"Forget it, never mind. You need a refill? Jackie, he needs a refill."

I look at him hard. He won't look back at me. He shifts on his stool.

I look away from him, into the mirror. I see Pauly's body on a steel table, the white sheet crumpled where his legs used to be. The medical examiner, her glasses pushed up on her forehead like that's where she thought her eyes were. *We don't think it's any other type of situation.*

We sit in silence for a while, watching commercials. The donation glass is right in front of me, and I stare at the few bucks inside it for a while. I feel like my head is going to explode and I want suddenly just to get the hell out of there. I stand, finish my drink, and stick my cigarettes in my suit coat pocket.

"Where are you going?"

"Gotta get back there."

"Hold on," says Sully, collecting his cigarettes. "I'll come with."

"No. Finish your beer." I nod to Jackie and the old guys.

Sully sighs, drops back onto his stool. "Toolie! Come back here," he whines. "Come on, man. Let me buy you another . . ."

* * *

My legs are numb, my footsteps thudding inside my head. Motors rattle past. I hear laughing, and when I look up, a group of kids shove past me, fighting their way up the street.

I stop at an empty lot surrounded by a fence. The lot is too small for a rink. But the houses behind it are ready to come down. I imagine going to their doors, making offers: *We'd like to build a community rink here in honor of Paul O'Toole.* In the front we'll have one of those life-size statues of him, maybe a giant version of his MVP All-State trophy. Guarding the net, stick poised. I grip the fence and peer through. There's a lot of people who'd be willing to donate. I'd go door-to-door if I had to. To hell with Jimmy and Ma. I could do it on my own. If there wasn't enough money here, I could go to Boston. A lot of people still remember Pauly on the ice. He was in the papers.

The snow inside the fence looks new, or at least a few shades whiter than the piles lining the street. When I was a kid I loved looking at the snow in the empty lots, still perfect, all the cans and wrappers hidden beneath whiteness. It always made me feel good, like there was a place safe from the rest of the world.

I shove the tip of my shoe in one of the fence rungs and heave myself up. I watched Pauly climb these fences a thousand times. If he saw a spot where the snow hadn't been touched, he'd jump the fence and have his feet be the first on it. An image of him comes back to me: parka unzipped, flapping behind him, his pants hanging out of his snow boots. I can hear his laugh. He runs circles through the lot, kicking up snow behind him.

Leave it be, Pauly! It looks nice like that.

Come on, Emmie, jump! What the hell are you waiting for?

I balance myself against the top of the fence, the tips of its metal triangles digging into me. My legs are shaking. He's wearing his old navy parka, the tear in the shoulder, the pilled polyester lining showing. I gave him that tear when we got in a fight on the way home from school once. He told Ma some other kid did it.

Are you just going to hang there like a pussy? Jump!

Stop it, Pauly! Stop it!

I watch him dance through the snow. Then I hear his voice, not like a memory, but as if he's honest-to-God standing on the sidewalk beneath me. A sore voice, an ugly voice: Didn't know you had it in you, little brother.

I try to shut it out. I focus on the snow.

What, I think, *we were supposed to just take all your shit whenever you felt like dropping by? As soon as the whole fucking world stopped revolving around you, you couldn't take it, could you?*

You know if you would have pressed it, Ma would have let me stay.

No, you're the one who fucked it all up, Pauly. You're the one who got into that car drunk and fucked it all up.

A car honks as it goes past and startles me. The lot is smooth again, and as I look out at it, I think, *I'm sorry, Pauly.* But just as quickly as I think it, it falls away, and

I'm left staring out at the empty white lot. I've never felt the kind of fear I feel right then, and I know, I realize, it's not the kind of fear that will ever pass. It's the kind of fear I saw in Pauly's face, the kind I see in Ma's; the kind that passes into doom. *No way, Pauly,* I think, *you're not taking me with you.*

Again, his voice:

I would've told her to go to hell if I had to.

"Yeah? Well, fuck you. Fuck you, Pauly."

My own voice startles me, and my feet give way. I slip down the fence and stumble onto the sidewalk, hearing the back of my suit coat rip open. When I stand I realize I'm shivering. I look up the street, wonder if anyone saw me or heard me. I brush the snow off my suit and start walking again.

I'm drunk is all. I have no idea how the hell long I've been gone, and I think of Ma. She's standing by the trophy display, holding mourners' hands. *Oh, yes, we'll find who did this to our Pauly.* She has her martyr and her villain, and after this is all over, I'll drive her to daily mass, where she'll go inside and pray in adoration of one and in redemption of the other. I stumble along, feeling the wind come through the tear in my jacket. I can't stop shaking from the cold, and I break into a run.

Outside Murphy's, the bums and cabbies have left, a couple of coffee cups sitting in the snow. The wake has emptied out but for a cluster of mourners. Murphy is chatting with Father Frank near the casket. Ma is packing her display up.

She sees me and continues packing. "Where the hell have you been?" she whispers.

"I needed some air."

"Some Flynn's air, no doubt."

"I'm sorry."

She doesn't answer, slides a rubber band around the ribbons.

"I was at Flynn's, having some beers."

"Well, good for you," she snaps. "I need you to bring me by Deluca's to pick up the platters for the open house. And we still need some buns for the cold cuts. Is that a rip in your jacket? For heaven's sake. What do you plan on wearing to the funeral? Your sweat suit?"

"Where's Jimmy?"

"They went to see Angela's mother. They'll be by later."

I collapse into a chair beside her. "Jackie put out a cup for Pauly's rink."

She huffs. "I can't think of a worse place to ask a man to part with his money. You won't be building any rink on nickels and dimes." After a second she glances at me. She feels bad for saying that, and I wait for her to follow it with something a little softer. When after a minute she still hasn't said anything, I say, "Everything was built on nickels and dimes, Ma."

"You're right. I guess it depends on how many of them you have." Then she says gently, "I wouldn't put it past you. You and your brother were always expert at nickel-and-diming people." We both try and laugh.

Across the room Murphy's mouth is moving; Father Frank has his arms crossed and rocks on his heels. Behind them, the casket. I reach out and pick up one of Pauly's trophies, run my finger over the little gold figure on top.

I start laughing suddenly. "Remember that time he got so pissed at me he threw all my underwear out the bedroom window into the tree?" It was winter or late fall, there weren't any leaves on the trees. My briefs like Christmas ornaments across the entire goddamn tree in the front yard. "And Dad out there on the ladder, flinging them off with a broom handle." I stood underneath the tree, trying to catch them. Thinking about it makes me laugh out loud.

Ma glances over at Father and Murphy and puts her finger over her lips.

"I didn't have a frigging"—she shoots me a look and I slap my hand over my mouth—"a single pair left. Not a one. He even got my dirty ones out of the hamper."

I wait for Ma to laugh, but she just says, "It wasn't your underwear. It was a couple of shirts."

"No, Ma, it was my underwear. It was my underwear. That was the whole gag."

"Pauly wouldn't have thrown a bunch of underwear in our front yard." She turns to Father. "Father, will you help yourself to the flowers? It's a shame for them to go to waste." She smiles and nods toward the arrangements.

"Yes, he did. That was the whole gag, remember, Ma?"

"Are you drunk? Because if you are, I'm not getting in

that car with you. I'll have Murphy or Father drive me home."

After a second, she continues fumbling with the trophies. She picks up the MVP All-State trophy, wipes it with her wad of Kleenex. "We have to get a move on. Deluca's closes in forty-five minutes."

"That was the whole gag. We all laughed about it, remember? Even Dad."

"No, I don't remember. But even if it had happened that way, you can bet your life your father wouldn't have found it funny."

My laughing has become crying, but I don't try to hide it. I wipe my face with my coat sleeve and look straight at her.

She studies my face for a moment and then glances at Father and Murphy and whispers, "You're drunk. How am I supposed to get through all the things we've got to do today with you drunk?"

"Ma—"

"We still have a million things to do before the funeral tomorrow. Did you clean the downstairs bathroom like I asked? With people in and out of there, I don't want it looking like hell." She undoes the pack of ribbons, begins to shuffle through them as if counting. "If we get a move on, maybe we'll have time to go up the street and see about a suit for you. Now, pull yourself together and start packing some of those flowers in the car. I thought your aunt Mary might like some of them. Take the roses."

I don't get up. I'm dizzy, the throb of my heart beating in my ears. I watch her pack the box, her chapped hands. When we were kids, after she'd yelled at us real bad, she'd come in at night and rub our backs. I'd lay there pretending to be sleeping, dreading the moment she'd stop and go to Pauly.

"Did you hear what I said?"

I put the trophy back down. Across the room, Father leans over and smells the flowers. "I'm more relieved than sad." I feel my throat tighten. "When they called and said he was dead, the first thing I thought was, Pauly's gone and done it."

She keeps up what she's doing for a minute. A few of the ribbons in her hands scatter to the floor. For a second she just stands there, looking down at them.

She kneels and begins fumbling with them; but all of a sudden she stands and goes behind the curtain at the rear of the room. Murphy and Father stop chatting and look over at me, confused. I lift my hand to them and follow her.

Behind the curtain is the room where we picked out Pauly's casket a couple of days ago. Murphy went around hoisting up the lids, telling us to touch the silk lining. Now Ma is at the rear of the room, her back to me. She looks small as a child standing there, and I feel sorry. But I don't say anything. Instead, I just stand there, watching her. Around us the caskets shine in the darkness.

Finally I say, "Ma, I'm sorry."

"I won't have any of this today. Deluca's closes in

forty-five minutes and I'm not waiting around for you to sober up. I'm not going to have a house full of people and no food." She wipes her face with her wad of Kleenex. She blows her nose and straightens herself.

"I'm sorry."

She dabs her temple with her tissue and starts moving toward the curtain. "Forget it. I'll have Father take me. I'll tell him my son is drunk at his own brother's funeral."

From beyond the curtain, Murphy: "Eily? Everything all right in there?"

"Fine, Pat, fine. I'll be right out."

"Can I get you anything?"

"No," Ma snaps. She corrects her tone. "Thank you though. I'll be right out." She is shaking, and she whispers as she begins to move past me, "Look at what you've done. You have no respect for me. And you sure as hell have no respect for your brother."

Then I hear myself speaking, and I realize what I'm saying only as it comes out of my mouth. "They told me it was a possibility."

She stops moving, looks up at me but doesn't say anything.

"They're not sure what happened. But they think it's possible he did it to himself."

"What the hell are you talking about? Who told you that? They said it was a homicide. They said it right to my face."

"They didn't want to hurt you."

"You're lying. You're drunk and you don't know what

the hell you're talking about." She waits for me to respond, and when I don't she says, "I'm not going to listen to this."

"He could have had a gun. And afterward somebody just took it. His wallet wasn't even taken—"

"Don't give me that. You don't know a goddamned thing. If they said that, they're liars. It's impossible."

I focus on the window and the gray light that comes through. Softly I say, "They didn't want to hurt you. But you need to know."

She drops her face in her hands. "It's impossible," she says. "They told me themselves. They looked right at me and told me themselves."

"Ma, he had nowhere to go."

"Don't give me that," she hisses. "What was I supposed to do? Tell me. He comes into my house, urinates all over everything, threatens to kill me. And a lot of help you were, I might add. If we had a man in the house it wouldn't have had to be that way."

"All we knew to do was love him, Ma. We couldn't do anything else."

After a moment she lifts her face to me. "Emmet," she says. Her eyes are alive with anguish. Beyond the curtain there's complete quiet, as if everyone has gone. It could have been true. That's what matters.

"I'm sorry, Ma." I reach out and set my hand awkwardly on her back. "It's not for sure. It's only a possibility."

She folds into herself, then shakes with sobbing. "It's not possible. I know he never would have—"

"He wasn't the same person near the end, Ma, you know that. He wasn't our Pauly."

It seems like a long time that I stand beside her, my hand on her back, and try to hush her. It's dusk now. Beyond the window the streetlights have come on. After a time she goes quiet and wipes her face. "We have to tell Father," she says quietly. "Even if it's only a possibility, Father's got to know."

"No, Ma," I say. "Father doesn't have to know. Nobody else ever has to know. Just you and me, Ma. Nobody else."

I reach for her, and she falls into me. For a second I tell myself that Pauly would've understood. I tell myself he'd forgive me. At that moment I vow that I'm going to build him his rink no matter what, and he won't be forgotten. But for now I hush Ma, my own whisper like a stranger's, and tell her we've got to pull ourselves together. Deluca's will be closing soon, and I'll take her where she needs to go, that we'll get through tomorrow and that everything will be okay.

RALPH
LOMBREGLIA

CASHMERE CHRISTMAS

Josephine couldn't recall if it was sacrilege to have leg of lamb on Christmas Eve, but considering that Jesus Christ was sometimes known as "The Lamb," it seemed potentially bad. When she invited her son and her former mother-in-law for Christmas Eve dinner, she'd been thinking about poaching a salmon. But then the meat man messed up a delivery to Ristorante Cantami, where Josephine cooked in Boston's North End, so she brought home an extra leg.

And then, pulling it out of the fridge this morning, it hit her: a leg of The Lamb.

What hooks they put in you! She hadn't been in a Catholic church in twenty years and here she was guilt-stricken over serving the wrong food on a certain day. All she wanted was one last holiday supper with her family, the only family she had, before she vanished forever—a decent-looking woman of thirty-nine giving her old bad life the slip and starting over in southern Florida. And suddenly she was battling ancient Catholic dragons rising out of her brain.

She stepped out to have a cigarette on her deck. She no longer smoked in the house and soon she wouldn't smoke at all. She might burn, but she wouldn't smoke. Not one filthy cig in the Sunshine State, that was her vow. It was drizzling, and fog had set in on account of the temperature rising so fast. She couldn't see the houses two streets away. The radio said it was warmer in Boston than in Tallahassee. Yes, the weather had done it again, switched to the Easter channel just in time for Christmas Eve. There hadn't been a white Christmas in the Boston area in ten years at least. Every year a blizzard hit in mid-December, and then for Christmas Eve it warmed up to fifty or fifty-five degrees and rained. In Josephine's girlhood they'd had a white Christmas every year. She was certain of it. When you were raised by a bunch of women who were all the brides of Christ, you remembered the birthday of the guy they were married to.

She toyed with the idea of calling her ex-husband, Sal. He was in prison for tax evasion, the only thing they could get him on. She could wish him a Merry Christmas and then hear his reaction to what she'd recently found. In the end she decided against it. It was too easy to picture him turning the whole thing around and making her look wrong, and he might even do worse than that. The man was capable of spooky insights into things. He would hear that she'd been cleaning out a closet, and with only that information he might unravel her mind like a ball of yarn and deduce that she was selling the house behind everyone's back and running away.

A week ago she'd been working on her son's old room, bagging up Ricky's old high-school shirts and pants for Goodwill. An odd velvety darkness remained in his closet after she'd emptied it out. Expecting to touch nothingness, she reached inside. It was not nothingness. It was Sal's black cashmere coat, hanging at the back of the closet in Ricky's old room. She and Sal had once had a terrible fight about this very garment—fifteen years ago, when he, a married guy in his late twenties with a child and no visible means of support, had purchased it while forbidding Josephine to buy things for herself, or for the house, or even for the kid. Now she was divorced two years and the man's black ghost had been there all the while. She slid the big coat along the closet pole into the light. Dust covered the padded shoulders like frost on a corpse standing up frozen outside. It hung lopsided on its wooden hanger, and when Josephine pulled one of its shoulders to straighten it out, she felt a funny weight on the coat's far side. She turned it and saw the pocket puckering open.

She knew it was a gun before she touched it, and then when she touched it she really knew, though she had never touched a gun before. There was a gun in the pocket of Sal's cashmere coat. With thumb and forefinger she lifted it by the handle. Was that what it was called, "the handle"?

She didn't think so. The grip, the stock, whatever. She assumed it was the very gun that Sal had once pointed at her during a fight, claiming later that it wasn't loaded, that he didn't even own bullets for it. She didn't know how to check if it was loaded now, and she'd undoubtedly kill herself if she tried. She dropped it back into the soft black pocket, where it disappeared so completely, with such perfect absence of sound, that she rapped the coat with her knuckles to see if it was really there.

With the bags of old clothes in her trunk she drove down the aluminum-sided, fake-bricked Broadway of Revere, Massachusetts, where Goodwill operated its donation trailer at a supermarket not far from Josephine's house. She had decided to dump the gun on those poor Christian charity workers. It would not be the first time they'd got one, Josephine was sure, and this way it would fall into semi-official hands; kids wouldn't pick it out of the trash somewhere.

When she arrived, other people were engaged in the holiday tradition of casting household discards upon the poor. Eight or nine cars had collected at odd, ad hoc angles in the parking lot as if they'd careened off each other in a terrible wreck, their drivers out standing on line. The man in charge was up there in the trailer just the way Josephine remembered—a formerly homeless or drunken man, one had to assume from the look of him, a man who knew better than most citizens the value of decent, warm clothing passed hand to hand—except with one important difference. He was holding a clipboard this time and checking off every item that everyone had.

She could not believe that Goodwill had chosen this Christmas to bring its operations into the twentieth century. Surely in checking in her things the man would put his hand directly on the unmistakable lump of the gun, or he would lift the cashmere coat to admire it, unfurling it like a black flag from which a pistol would cascade to the ground and discharge, killing him, or Josephine, or some innocent bystander. She parked her patched-up Honda and thought about sneaking the weapon out of the coat. Then she saw the wisdom of removing the coat from her offerings altogether. An observer would see only a woman having second thoughts about donating a cashmere coat—a snooty woman willing to give to the poor but never her very best things, never something that could be considered finery. She pulled the coat from its bag and left it in the trunk, and then gave unto others the clothes worn by her son before he became a lying thief. And then she stamped back to her chalky, gray, unlovely automobile and drove away beneath the red garlands of Broadway, with her black cashmere coat and her possibly loaded firearm.

She'd had the gun a week now and still didn't know if it had bullets in it. It was in her locker at work. She was waiting for the chance to show it to Roberto, one of her fellow chefs at Ristorante Cantami. Roberto was the type to know about guns. In her mind the gun was already one of Roberto's cherished possessions, though she kept having fleeting visions of herself alone on the road to Boca Raton with a gun to wave around.

Most Italian mothers-in-law considered their sons' ex-wives to be dead, but Josephine's divorce had made her and Camilla closer than ever. And that, thought Josephine, was why you had to take care of your health. In the end you found out who really loved you, but you had to live that long. From her front door she watched the old lady emerge from a yellow cab at the curb, a tiny refugee from a Sicilian hill town dressed in black as always, still in mourning for Gaetano after fifteen years. Ricky the fledgling hoodlum was already on the sidewalk with his girlfriend, Charlene. To his credit he tried to help his grandmother out of the cab, but she swatted him with her cane. Josephine wondered how much money her son had gambled on sporting events today, and where he had gotten that money, and what he had flowing in his veins along with the blood. Maybe in honor of Christmas he was on angel dust.

She opened her door and called, "Merry Christmas!" When her guests came in, she took their coats in the hall. She did not think that Ricky was actually selling Charlene, but you wouldn't know it from Charlene's hair and makeup and tight red crushed-velvet dress, or from Ricky's own little mustache and gold jewelry and shiny suit.

Camilla watched them stroll into Josephine's living room. "What's God think?" she asked Josephine.

"He hasn't confided in me lately," Josephine said.

She was playing her one and only holiday CD, some tinkly stringed instruments doing a New Age Christmas-carol medley with no discernible beginning or end. It made the house feel like a shopping mall, but a high-end mall with superior stores. Into this hypnotic festivity she carried a tray of drinks. She'd already had half a bottle of Chardonnay while preparing dinner, but she had another glass anyway. In Florida she was drinking only carbonated spring water with juice from oranges and grapefruits grown fifty feet from wherever she was sitting, and then she was lying in the sun until cosmic rays brought the glow of those fruit spritzers to the surface of her skin.

They toasted the season in the pulsing pastel light of Josephine's tree, a little four-foot job from the Boy Scouts of Revere. Its blinking reminded her of roadside distress. On the stereo the dulcimers and mandolins were plucking out a shimmery "Silent Night," clusters of notes issuing from the speakers like a glittering astral garment worn collectively by the people in the room. Draped in it, Josephine drifted away and returned with a long dry-cleaning bag.

Charlene rose to help her lift the plastic. "Wow!" she said when she saw what was underneath—a beautiful black cashmere coat.

"What's that?" said Ricky, sitting up straight.

"What's it look like?" said Charlene. "A cashmere coat, you lucky dog."

"It's not a Christmas present," Josephine said. "It's a hand-me-down. It belonged to Ricky's father." She walked over and held the coat before her son on the sofa. She'd had it cleaned. Its nap had come up better than she'd expected, restored to a lustrous black. It didn't look used at all except that the right side pocket still drooped a little from the weight of the gun.

Ricky stared into the darkness of the coat.

"Do you remember your father wearing it?" asked Josephine.

"I guess so."

"Do you like it?"

"Yeah, it's nice."

"Would you mind standing up?"

With his mother holding one side of the coat and his sweetheart holding the other, young Richard was enfolded in his heirloom mantle of black cashmere as a prince might have been vested in the olden times.

"You look just like him," said Camilla.

"I'm taking that as a compliment," said Ricky.

It was true, and Josephine had not braced herself for it. The coat was magic—bad magic that you couldn't stop once you'd played with it. She and Camilla had aged fifteen years, but here was Sal just as he'd been back then.

Ricky, in fact, seemed not to like the coat. He stood rotating his head like some military device designed to survey the room while avoiding the heat of human faces.

"What do you think?" Charlene asked.

"It's too big."

"We can have it taken in."

"It's not my style."

"What?" said Charlene. "It is so. You have lots of things that would go with a classy coat like this." She led him out to the oval mirror in the hall. "A hat would tie it all together," she called to Josephine.

"A black hat," said Josephine.

"I have a hat," said Ricky.

"You have a ski mask," said Charlene.

"Dad's gonna need a warm coat when he gets out," said Ricky.

"That coat and another coat just like it," said Josephine.

"He lost weight in the joint."

"Not that much weight he didn't."

Josephine asked everyone to hold hands at the table while she recited a prayer she remembered from her girlhood with the nuns. Privately, she prayed that her roast was not the transubstantiated haunch of the Savior, or that if it was, no doom would descend on them for eating it. Either her prayer was irrelevant or it worked. She carved and served her leg of lamb and the lights stayed on. Camilla and Ricky had second helpings and the roof stayed where it was. Charlene didn't eat the lamb at all, but not for religious reasons. She thought it was too garlicky. Then she hit the broccoli rabe and found out what garlic was all about. The poor girl ended up having wild rice and yams for dinner, with two more vodka tonics. She didn't care for the taste of wine. Josephine tried to imagine her married to Ricky—they seemed to be moving in that direction. Josephine was moving in a direction too. South.

She was pleased with her meal. The lamb was tender and flavorful, the greens crisp and zesty, the wine spicy and round. She served homemade apple tart with real whipped cream for dessert, and dazzled her humble company with a fine Cognac for the finish. Then she became even more expansive and announced that she would drive everyone home herself.

Because she was tired and had to take Ricky and Charlene all the way to Lynn, the next town up the coast, she used the shortcut to Camilla's house on the other side of Revere. It went behind the elementary school on the hill and then through a dark, wooded stretch of bumpy road near the ocean. Josephine lived in a city by the sea, but she had long ago ceased going to the beach. Revere Beach was closed half the time on account of pollution, and when it was open it was full of thugs and the water was too cold to swim in anyway. In Florida people didn't leave beer cans and bullet casings on the sand, and the waves were warm and didn't contain human waste and drug syringes. She'd never been to Florida, but she'd seen it in magazines. It started to rain again. She flipped the wipers to high. The fog had lifted near the water, but the black ocean and the dark woods and the windswept rain were almost as bad as fog. She could scarcely tell where she was. "I can't believe this is Christmas Eve," she said.

"And next week there'll be a foot of snow on the ground," said Ricky.

"I know. Doesn't it kill you? They can't let us have a white Christmas."

"Who's 'they'?" said Ricky.

"Never mind."

"Maybe we should all move to Florida," Charlene said.

Josephine hit her brakes and the car fishtailed across the road. Nobody, nobody, nobody knew about that—except Camilla in whom she'd confided, and who was now clutching the dashboard and looking scared, but not guilty.

"What happened?" said Ricky.

"Nothing," said Josephine. "Something ran in front of me." She straightened out the car and drove along more slowly. She glanced at Charlene in the rearview mirror. "Florida, huh? Why should we all move to Florida?"

"Isn't that where people go to get away from this weather?"

"Not always. They go to California too."

"Not as much as Florida."

"They go to the islands," said Josephine.

"To live? They do not."

"You could have said, 'Maybe we should all move to Arizona.' "

"Maybe *you* should move to Arizona," said Ricky.

Josephine twisted around. "Who said I was moving anywhere?"

"Nobody. You have a few drinks and you start nitpicking."

"You're accusing somebody else of being stoned?" Her wheels hit the graveled shoulder.

"Josephine!" shouted Camilla.

"Stop the car," said Ricky. "I wanna drive."

"Sure, with your license revoked. All I'm saying is let's have some variety. You talk about winter and the first thing anybody says is Florida."

"It's a conspiracy to brainwash people," Ricky said.

"Are you making fun of me?" said Josephine.

A wet black mass slapped onto the windshield, a black hat or fabric purse or headband or something, and got caught in the wipers and started swiping across the glass in front of Josephine's face. She slammed the brakes and the car skidded around in a circle and stopped sideways in the middle of the road. Her first thought was that Ricky had ripped a cashmere lapel from the coat and thrown it at her, but that made no sense because Ricky was in the car. Everyone was yelling, like this proved she was incompetent to drive—like anybody could drive with a wad of wet black garbage on her windshield. She got out in the rain. The sky was conducting a massive energy-transfer with the sea. The black thing was swinging back and forth in the driver's-side wiper, and when she grabbed for it she screamed and jumped back in the car. "It's alive! It's some kind of animal!"

Ricky got out from the backseat and banged on the driver's window until Josephine rolled it down. "Shut off the wipers," he said.

She did that, and then Charlene and Camilla started screaming. It was a bat. One wing was stuck under the wiper and the other was slapping against the glass. Ricky raised the wiper and the bat tried to fly away, but it couldn't fly anymore and tumbled instead onto the hot hood of the car, where raindrops made puffs of steam all around it.

"Great. Now we're cooking the poor thing," Josephine called out.

"I'm not the one who hit it," said Ricky.

"I didn't hit anything!" she called as he walked past her window again. "It flew right into me!"

He reappeared in the windshield with the cashmere coat in his hands. He spread it open so that for a moment he looked like a gigantic bat himself. Then he scooped up the little bat in the coat.

"You're not bringing that in here!" Charlene exclaimed.

"I'm not?" He got back in his seat.

"Take me home!" said Camilla.

Josephine put the car in gear and straightened it out. The bat was making horrific squealing sounds from the coat on Ricky's lap.

"Don't let it bite you, Ricky!" said Charlene, squeezing herself against her passenger door. "They have rabies!"

"They suck your blood!" said Camilla.

* * *

Josephine reached Camilla's house and shut off the car.

"We're going in herc?" asked Charlene.

"Would you rather take the bat to your place?" said Josephine.

"I don't want no bat!" said Camilla.

"It's just visiting, Ma," said Josephine. She and Ricky got out. "How's our buddy?" she asked.

"Freaked. He's staring at me and licking his lips."

"You could have been a vet, you know. You always loved animals."

"That's because I'm an animal myself, Mom."

She had called him an animal a few times in recent years, when he got busted for stealing cars, for drugs, for larceny, and when he tossed on the final straw—stealing from his own mother.

"I was being sincere, Ricky. Remember when you helped Missy have her puppies behind the couch?"

"Yeah. I buried Missy too."

"I'm trying to remember the happy things."

Josephine unlocked Camilla's front door and Ricky followed her inside with the bat in the coat. The house was too hot and smelled like an old person living alone. As on every other visit to Camilla's, Josephine saw new knickknacks and new pictures of the Pope.

"How about telling me what we're doing," Ricky said.

Josephine got out the big Boston phone book. "I'm calling for a bat consultation."

"Calling who? It's Christmas Eve."

She dialed and held the phone to her ear. "I raised you, right? You didn't raise me. When you get finished raising somebody, I'll check how smart you are."

She was calling Angell Memorial, the famous Boston animal hospital. Hospitals didn't close for Christmas, and this place was like the Mayo Clinic for pets. They had experimental therapies and cancer drugs you couldn't get for human beings. The dogs and cats of millionaires probably got heart transplants there. And why not? thought Josephine. They deserved it more than people did.

Camilla and Charlene came in from outside, looking like they'd had a chat, unlikely as that seemed. "We think you should call the cops," Charlene said.

"The cops?" said Ricky. "How about the FBI? Why don't you call some astronauts while you're at it?"

Somebody picked up at Angell Memorial. "A bat flew into my car," Josephine told the woman on the phone.

"Leave the doors open and it'll fly back out," the woman said.

Josephine laughed through her nose. "That's like a Henny Youngman routine." The woman didn't understand. "I guess you get a lot of weird calls."

"We see the full range of occurrences," said the woman.

Josephine explained her own occurrence with less ambiguity than before. Because it involved an injured creature from the great outdoors, she was given the number of the MSPCA—an agency, not a hospital, and thus a place that she was certain would not be open on Christmas Eve. But she dialed it and punched numbers at the recorded promptings. On the sofa Ricky had the cashmere coat open to examine the bat. "What's what?" she asked him.

"One wing is kind of ripped. Bones don't feel broken, though."

"Ricky, if you get bit by that bat I'm gonna freak," said Charlene.

A woman came on the phone. Josephine said, "I can't believe you're there on Christmas Eve."

"The holidays are an at-risk time for animals," the woman said.

"You should see what they're like for people," said Josephine.

"That was my point," said the woman.

Josephine described the situation.

"I bet it likes that cashmere coat," the woman said. "The warm weather is what woke the bat up in the first place. The bat is supposed to be hibernating, but he got a rogue signal from his environment."

"My son says it's struggling and hurting itself even more."

"Tell your son the cashmere coat needs to be in the fridge."

The words *your son* on the lips of a sensible young woman sent a yearning through Josephine like a glandular secretion. But there was nothing to be done. Life had taken its course. "The fridge?"

"You can induce torpor by getting it cold. That's what our people do when they work with bats. Pop 'em in the fridge. They drop right off."

Josephine repeated this information to Ricky, who nodded his head as if he knew it already, having studied bats in some veterinary college that held classes in his mind. Camilla had brought out supplies. Ricky was applying antibiotic cream to the bat's wounded wing and offering it water from a bathroom Dixie cup. He said, "Tell her we don't want the bat to drop off. We want the bat to fly."

Josephine told the woman.

"Well, then, keep him in the cashmere cave," the woman said. "Get him nice and toasty. Little guy'll fly."

Ricky said, "Ask her if it can find its way home."

The woman heard that. "They have a great sense of direction," she said.

"And if he doesn't fly?"

"Call me back," said the woman, and hung up the phone.

"Come on, everybody," said Josephine. "Let's release Dracula here. We're doing this on the wrong holiday. This should be Halloween. Except Halloween would be colder."

They went outside and assembled on Camilla's tiny front lawn in the yellow glow of the black lamppost rising from her walk. The Christmas Eve weather now resembled bad summer vacation luck on the coast of Maine—dank and vaguely chilly, encased in dense mist.

Ricky laid the coat on the grass. "Merry Christmas!" he said, and opened it like a magician making a bat disappear—which, indeed, he had become. There was no bat inside. There was bat vomit in the coat, or bat shit, or both, but no bat—not in the coat, or on the ground, or anywhere in the misty sky.

"Where the hell's the bat?" said Josephine.

"I don't know," said Ricky, picking up the coat and turning it around. "I don't believe it. I lost the bat."

"He's in my house!" Camilla cried.

"No," said Josephine, "I saw him in the coat when we walked outside."

"Everything's black," said Charlene. "Black coat, black bat, black sky."

"Somebody would have seen something," said Ricky. He wandered into the darkness beyond the glow of the lamp. "Did I drop it and kick it into the shrubs?"

"I doubt it," said Josephine, but she followed him anyway.

"Where's my gun?" Ricky asked her softly.

"What?" she whispered back.

"My gun. What did you do with it?"

"What gun? You had a gun?"

"You know what gun."

Out on the lamplit lawn Charlene said, "Houdini the bat," and all at once the true meaning of Christmas suffused Josephine's brain. The reason you had Jesus and Santa for the same holiday was that they were different ways of telling the same story. A magical creature arrives and brings you something you don't deserve, to teach you the lesson that deserving is beside the point. Nobody deserves anything, everybody deserves everything. She had the overwhelming conviction, undeserving as she was, that when she opened her basement locker at Ristorante Cantami, the pistol would not be there.

"Ricky," she whispered. "What about this? What if the bat was actually your gun? Like the wine turning into the blood? Say your gun turned into a bat as a sign that guns are bad, and then it disappeared. Like Santa Claus."

"You are getting really weird," said Ricky.

"You wouldn't say that if you went to Catholic school like me. You don't believe in anything. That's your problem. That's where I went wrong. I should have sent you to the sisters."

"Did you take it to the restaurant? It's at the restaurant, isn't it?"

"I just told you," she said, shooting her hand like a bat. "Zoom."

"I want it back."

She angled her hand at the sky. "Talk to Heaven."

She took the coat off his arm and stepped into the light where Camilla and Charlene were still looking on the grass for the bat. She shook the coat. No bat fell out. But a bat had once been in there, no question. "Are you gonna wear this?" she asked Ricky. "If you're gonna wear it, I'll get it cleaned."

"I'd like to wear it right now," said Ricky. "Get me a hat that makes things disappear and I'll wear that too."

"Houdini's coat and hat," said Charlene.

"Houdini would be a picnic," said Josephine. "I think that bat was Jesus."

"I can't believe how religious you are," said Charlene.

"I can't either," said Josephine.

She kissed Camilla good-night and then opened her trunk and tossed in the coat. "Let's go, you two," she said, and started her car, thinking about how this story would now enter family lore—The Bat That Disappeared on Christmas Eve—to be marveled over every year yet never truly understood, and made more incorrect with each retelling. But that wasn't the scary thing. The scary thing was that this was the way it was with every story ever told, as when you saw your own neighborhood on the nightly news and the place they were showing wasn't your neighborhood at all.

STEWART
O'NAN

20 BURGERS

for Andre Dubus

The Fat Man signs followed them along 80, through the counties they'd beaten to make regionals—Lycoming, Montour, Luzerne. It was wet, December, dusk, just about dinnertime. They were playing Susquehanna in Scranton to go to states, and Kerry thought she should have packed more balls. In practice everyone had to have one. You only got fifteen minutes between games, and it was important to know the floor, to get a feel for the key, to test the back of the glass. Coach didn't like to see any empty hands. Last month Kerry had culled the old, bulgy leather ones, thinking the season was pretty much over. Now she was worried she wouldn't have enough.

They burrowed through the fog in the cuts above Bloomsburg, under hawks circling high over roadkill, past bare stands of pine ravaged by salt. In back the subs were singing "John Jacob Jingleheimerschmidt," the starters catnapping, annoyed. Coach slept under her trench coat, her toes poking out. They weren't supposed to win; they weren't even supposed to go this far. There was no boasting the way there'd been at midseason, no jive rhymes or bad raps about the other team. Kerry put a hand to the chilly window. The rocks were covered with lovers' graffiti. They crested the hill and started the long drop into the same brown plain of farms and forests. It was drizzling, and the billboard was lit, a gigantic man's face like a balloon.

20 BURGERS, it said, AND YOUR BUS EATS FREE!

Ketchup exploded from the one in his fist, little red exclamation points.

"That's so disgusting," Moriah said beside her.

Kerry watched the rain, the way it disappeared, then was suddenly there again. She was going to have to eat them, she knew. She was the only one on the bus capable. She'd been dreading it since they clinched. She knew the route from visiting Gram in Throop; she'd mulled the challenge for years as a little kid.

"The Fat Man's for dinner?" Coach asked.

The bus gave a mutter of assent, and she settled again.

So, Kerry thought, no way out of it now.

"I wonder how big they are," Moriah said. She was thin, with braces that made her jaw prominent. They were comanagers, but Moriah was a friend of Stacey Gaither, and lettered in cross-country in the spring. Kerry was just doing it because she liked hoops, probably because of

Matt. He'd only been on the JV but he was the star; they'd dedicated the season to him after the surgery didn't work. Her mother liked to think that that was when she started getting fat, but she was big before then. Her mother stored her outsized jeans in airtight Rubbermaid containers in the basement, even after Kerry told her not to bother. They were still there, the twelves and fourteens; this winter she was pushing 1X stretchies.

"Regular size," Kerry said. "Like McDonald's. Plus you have to eat a side of fries and a milkshake."

"Twenty. I couldn't eat five of them."

"Yeah, you could. Easy."

"How many did Scott Markham eat?"

"Twenty-two," Kerry said.

Everyone knew the story. Scott was the manager of the boys' team. He was retarded, and huge, with a blind eye that never closed, and last year before regionals he'd eaten twenty-two and they beat Lackawanna in front of their own home crowd. After that, Beaver Falls was nothing; they broke a hundred with a minute left. Outside of town, when you got off 80, there was a sign that said Milesburg was the home of the State Champion Millers. In the trophy case there was a picture with Scott sitting in front of the team, a ball in his lap.

There was a picture of Matt in the case, too, skinny in his uniform, number fourteen. Freshman year her teachers asked if they were related; now they just called her name, checked off the box. She knew they did the arithmetic in their heads, that they knew she was just three years behind him, that she was the only one her parents had left now. She knew they thought it was a bad trade, Matt for her, the athlete for the fat girl, the funny one for the nut. What could she say: they were right.

The picture of Matt was right next to the one of the State Champs. It was the team he would have been on, probably would have captained it. Once her dad even said, "Think how good they would have been." Everyone said it. Not Mom, but everyone else.

Everyone loved Scott Markham after that. At parties people sat with him when they were tired of dancing, and when he got a job at the Friendly's downtown, all the seniors started hanging out there. Before that, everyone called him Snot, and Popeye. Now they called him Mr. Twenty-two, and he wore his letter jacket everywhere.

"They say he didn't even throw up," Moriah said, with a mix of admiration and horror.

"You'd have to," Kerry said, as if she'd thought about it.

She had. The key, she thought, was squishing the bread. That and putting just enough ketchup on so they didn't get dry. You didn't have to have anything on them, not even cheese.

She'd heard that Scott Markham stacked the first five together in one bun, then used the milkshake to wash down the extra bread.

"Think if you didn't," Moriah said, and stuck out her tongue.

"We'll see," Kerry said.

"Get out," Moriah said. "You're *not* gonna."

"You don't think so?"

"Get *out*!" She turned in her seat to read Kerry's face better, and smiled so her braces showed. "Oh my God, oh my God," she said, and popped up so she could broadcast to the back rows: "Kerry's going to do it, Kerry's going to eat twenty burgers!"

Silence.

"Right," a skeptic said.

It took them a minute to realize she was serious.

"You trying to inspire us?" Stacey Gaither asked, half mockingly. She'd been quiet the whole ride. She was their starting center, and Susquehanna's was All-State.

"No girl's ever done it," Kerry said.

"No *woman*," said Coach from under her trench coat, and they cheered.

"I'll be the first," Kerry said, already regretting it, but it got another cheer. She was surprised how much she liked the applause. It went through her like a chill, tightening everything, getting her blood up.

"You sure you want to do this?" Coach asked.

"I'm sure." She nodded solemnly.

The girls in back, even Stacey, began to chant her name—"Ker-ry, Ker-ry"—and Moriah took her wrist and raised her arm in the air as if she'd already won. Kerry waved, thinking it was better than letting them talk her into it. This, at least, would be on her terms. And even if that wasn't completely true, she was pleased to be the object of something other than pity. Not love, no. Not even friendship. She was a nut, okay, but she wasn't stupid.

1

They brought the first one out on a regular plate, with fries, and a chocolate shake in a heavy parfait glass. On each side of Kerry there was an empty chair so the waitress could bring new plates and get rid of the old ones. Coach sat across from her, holding her hands out as if signaling Kerry to slow down. The sheet the rules were on was speckled from being photocopied so often. You had an hour, and you weren't allowed to go to the bathroom.

"Duh," Moriah said. "Anyone could do it that way."

Kerry squeezed the bun and ate the first burger in four equal bites.

"One!" everyone said.

2

They served her first, so the other girls sipped their water and watched. The last time Kerry had been here, they were coming back from the hospital. It was just a visit, but her mom decided to stay overnight, and her dad liked the Fat Man, thought of it as a charming local joke.

It hadn't changed since then. There was a huge snifter of miniature peppermint patties at the register. The chairs were heavy and the carpet was a dark red that hid spills. Near the ceiling a train puffed around the room on a canted track, the clash of its wheels disappearing after a few minutes, becoming one with the Muzak and chatter. Most of the people were older and didn't pay it any attention.

Her dad got a booth for the two of them. She was thirteen, and he knew not to help her order; her mom still did, pointing out salads, saying things like "Remember those nice asparagus last spring? They have that grilled chicken you like."

They ordered and the waitress went to get their drinks. "Kerr," her dad said, and laid his hand between the bread and butter plates, palm up. She was supposed to take it, and then they'd talk, briefly but seriously, about Matt, and what might happen.

On the wall the train hurried along, and she imagined herself on it, hurtling through tunnels and perfect Christmas villages covered with wads of cotton snow. The houses glowed, and in the windows stood motionless silhouettes, like the clerks at the gas stations outside of Milesburg, bent over their papers while Kerry and her dad moved through the night.

She laid her hand in his, and he covered it.

3

She asked for ketchup, remembering Scott Markham.

Coach waved the waitress over, and in a minute she came back with a bottle of Heinz. It took too long to pour, and Coach stuck a knife up the neck.

Kerry turned the burger in her hands like a wheel, keeping the same rhythm of four precise bites. Already it seemed she was slowing, the taste a hook in her throat. She paused and focused on the ketchup bottle, the pickle and the address of the company.

In sixth grade the big field trip was to the Heinz plant in Pittsburgh. They got to see Three Rivers, where the Steelers played, and the Andy Warhol Museum, but the highlight was seeing people completely dressed in plastic watch machines make ketchup. You were on a catwalk high above the floor so you could see the big vats. The guide had to use a bullhorn. At the end they gave you a box of their products—a miniature bottle of ketchup, a jar of relish—and a green pin in the shape of a pickle. Matt had one from the time he went, and when Kerry got hers, he was the first one she showed it to.

"So?" he said.

"It's just like yours," she said.

"And?"

4

The ketchup made it easier; it changed the taste. Two new waitresses were taking the other girls' orders. Moriah had the salad bar, which pissed Kerry off. She'd come back with a few scraps of lettuce and pick at it, then leave half. As if it wasn't obvious. But everyone stared at Kerry and no one said anything about Moriah, how her wrists were just knobs, how she used to have boobs. In the hall it was common for boys to say mean things to Kerry; sometimes they just mooed. Last week Moriah broke up with Tim Bennett, and this Friday she was going to see the new *Star Wars* with Barry Fuelgraff.

Kerry turned the wheel.

"Four!" everyone said.

5

The first waitress brought the next four arranged on a plate. Her name was Christine, and her hair was honey colored and pulled back in a tie-dyed scrunchie.

"Four more," she said, and Kerry couldn't tell if she was making fun of her.

She didn't look anything like Christine Lamoreaux, who was tiny and dark and wore red all the time. Matt always called her Tina, but no one else did. She was a year behind him, but pretty, so it made sense. After Matt died, everyone felt sorry for her, but she had her girlfriends who hung out in the parking lot, and by next spring she was going with Jeff Kunz, who everyone liked because he worked with deaf kids at the Rehab and did sign language for their cable show.

It didn't bother Kerry. Matt had only been going out with her a few weeks; it didn't really mean anything, just some making out in the back of their station wagon, maybe a hand down his pants. It wasn't like Diane Wolfson, who would do anything.

But Kerry remembered going to see Matt around

Thanksgiving and finding Christine in his room, sitting by his pillow, filling him in on *General Hospital*, all the characters and story lines and gossip, and Kerry thought that it wasn't right, that that was her job.

6

Don't rush your food, her mother always said. Leave some room; you should still be a little hungry when you leave the table. Chew your food, don't inhale it. Slow down; there's enough for everyone.

7

The rest of their food came, and Coach and Moriah and a few other girls set off for the salad bar, leaving Stacey Gaither across from her. She'd ordered a taco salad, the bowl a puffed tortilla shell, a thousand calories all by itself. Kerry watched to see if she'd eat it.

"Don't stop now," Stacey said, and dug in, snapping a piece off.

She had long, almost white hair, and you could barely see her eyebrows. Under the basket she was impossible to move, all elbows and shoulders. She was the tallest on the team, and once, handing out towels in the shower, Kerry saw she was lopsided, one high, slim, and perfect, the other heavy and pointing toward the floor. Still, it seemed to make her more beautiful to Kerry, more vulnerable, and she hoarded this vision of her. That and the one time she'd seen her in a dress, at last year's awards dinner.

It wasn't a crush, it wasn't like she was gay or anything, she just liked the way Stacey looked, her long legs, the dish of her hips. She'd heard the other girls say it after dinner: Stacey could be really pretty if she tried. It was familiar; her mom used to say the same thing about her.

Kerry watched her digging into her taco salad, a fleck of lettuce on her lower lip.

Stacey caught her watching, and for a second Kerry was sure she knew. The train raced into the other room.

"Hey," Stacey said, "you're not quitting, are you?"

8

They came back from the salad bar, laughing.

"How we doing?" Coach asked, and Stacey told her eight.

"Almost halfway," Moriah said, trying to be a cheerleader. She had a scattering of leaves on her plate, a few carrot sticks, a crescent of red pepper, dressing on the side in a tiny NyQuil cup.

Last Sunday Kerry had seen a movie on TV about a girl with bulimia. It was a true story; the girl who played her was the girl who'd survived it in real life, and Kerry wondered how that felt. Like she'd won, maybe.

There was a scene in a graveyard when she went to visit a friend that died. It was a sunny day, and the star knelt down and put some flowers right near the stone like a pillow and said, "I'm sorry," like it was her fault.

The last time they went to Matt's grave, her mom was all upset because the cemetery hadn't put flowers on it like they were supposed to.

"It's all right," her dad said.

"It is *not* all right," her mom said. "What are we paying them for if they're not going to do it? I'll come up here myself and do it if they're not going to. Someone is going to remember him, damn it. My son is *not* going to be forgotten."

"All right," her dad said, "all right. *I* will take care of it, okay? I'll talk to them Monday morning. Now can we just have a nice visit for once?"

Kerry looked off past the rows of graves and through the leafless trees and down over the river and the gray streets of Milesburg. You could see their house from here, just the chimney; it was one reason why they bought the plot, why they faced it this way, as if Matt could sit up and look down on the town. As if that might comfort him.

9

They ate, all of them, pausing to watch her. Dinner would be free if she did it, but none of them ordered anything big. It wasn't because they doubted her; they had to play in two hours.

She chewed, slipping in a french fry, taking a little sip of the shake. Moriah rearranged the food on her plate like some kind of puzzle. Stacey cracked pieces off the shell. She wasn't beautiful the way people on TV were. Maybe her legs, like a razor commercial.

Moriah's eyes were. And Christine Lamoreaux's lips. Perfect, just the right size, that sexy thickness.

Sometimes in the mirror Kerry would squint to see if she was beautiful.

"You've got a pretty face," her mom said. "If you just lost some of that weight."

Maybe, she thought.

But then in the hall she'd pass someone like Stephanie Arnold in one of her sweaters, or Gina Barratieri in a mini, and the answer was clear. Nothing was going to save her.

10

"Halfway," Moriah said.

"She'll be halfway when she finishes this one," Stacey corrected her.

"You okay?" Coach asked.

Kerry nodded and tapped her watch. It had only been twenty minutes.

"Pace yourself," Coach said, and Kerry nodded again. It all tasted the same now. People leaving looked over at her, fascinated.

Go ahead and stare, she thought.

"You can do it," a bald man in a parka said, and clapped his gloved hands. When he left, a cold gust of wind chilled her ankles, and she thought of visiting Matt, the wind on the hill.

The day was a good week away, but she could feel it coming up. Her mom talked about him less, as if saving her grief for the anniversary, like hiding Christmas presents. Her dad rarely mentioned him, slipped, once a month let his name peek out of his mouth. His silence made it plain that he was thinking of him. Watching the Steelers win late, he didn't have to say, "Matt would have loved this." He just turned to her and said, "Great game, huh?" and she agreed.

No one called it The Anniversary. No one said that the house had to be quiet all day, or that she couldn't turn her boom box on (it was his, as were half her CDs—her Smashing Pumpkins and STP bootlegs, her Screaming Trees). No one had to say how many years it was this year. They got in the car, they got out, they got back in. The cemetery was actually the easy part.

11

"*Now* it's halfway," Moriah said. She had a piece of something stuck in her braces, and Kerry was glad she didn't have to tell her.

The burgers seemed to weigh more, and they were cold from sitting on the plate, waiting for her.

Some of the salad eaters were going up for more. It was all you can eat. A challenge lurked in the words, in the way they went together.

At home she ate cookies—Oreos and Nutterbutters—until her mom stopped buying them. She came home on the bus and threw her backpack on the couch and went straight for the cupboard, then the fridge to see if there was any milk. She spread the morning paper out and read all the good sections—the comics, Ann Landers, the horoscope. When her mom cut her off, she stopped at the Minit Mart, where they had goldfish and Ho Hos, mini-Ritzes with peanut butter. She threw the boxes down the sewer on her way up Bessemer, before she turned the corner.

But that was early, those were the first binges. Matt was still alive then, still waiting for them above Scranton in his room that overlooked the cloverleaf and the mall beyond it. So it wasn't about him. It was about her.

She couldn't remember, but she thought her mom told her about dogs. Humans know when to stop eating, she said. Not dogs. Dogs will eat till the food's all gone.

Okay, Kerry thought, maybe that was true. But maybe it was like andrenaline, too, the way people could pick up cars that had fallen on loved ones. Maybe the body was a mystery, she wanted to tell her mother, how emotions controlled it. You'd be amazed how much you could eat when you had to.

12

The others were almost done. She was slowing down, she could feel it, and wolfed the one in her hand.

After Matt went into the hospital, her mom had to stop

her from bolting her dinner and rushing upstairs. They needed this time together as a family. They needed to talk. They understood she was frightened, that she needed to know what was going on.

His room was the same, his bed made, his MVP trophy from the JV tournament in Reading on top of his dresser. Ribbons from swimming. The Game Boy he never let her use. Kurt Cobain gazed down sorrowfully from the wall, and she felt watched the way she did when, picturing Stacey Gaither, she loved herself in the tub, the briefest ecstasy giving way to disgust at her ugliness.

What was new in her room?

Nothing. Nothing at all.

13

Another quick one before the rest of them finished, in three big bites. It filled her cheeks. Coach looked over, worried.

She'd seen the look so often that she no longer made a face back at it. It was the look they gave her on line at the cafeteria, or when she didn't have an answer in class. They had theories about how she would never get over it. They looked at her as if she were sick, as if, like his cancer, Matt lived within her, eating Kerry from the inside out.

They were wrong. All she had to do was wait. In a year she would be off to college—they could afford Penn State—and all of this would be history. She'd never tell anyone, or maybe just her best friend, someone she was serious about.

"I had a brother once," she'd say, but nothing would change between them; it would only deepen things, be just a little extra part of her. It would be their secret.

14

No one ordered dessert; only Coach wanted coffee. She tipped her watch to show Kerry there was a half hour left. It was dark out now, and a trucker came in slapping snow off his Mack hat. So her mom would finally have her white Christmas. She'd been talking about it for weeks, like a little kid. It meant so much to her for things to be perfect.

Lately she'd returned to the church, slipped out of the house before the Sunday paper came, joined the old Polish ladies with their hair pinned up under babushkas, waddling up the aisles like geese. Kerry hadn't been since she was a kid, but she could still feel the cold stone on her knees, still see the flickering grottoes hiding behind pillars. The hymnals smelled of dust. Her mom lifted her rosary from her purse.

At home her dad lingered over the sports, drove deep into the opinion section. When her mom came back, happy, whipping her good gloves off, ready to make lunch, he retreated to the TV room and soaked in the day's slate of games, only breaking for supper. And then the next morning he was gone, off to the warehouse, free of them for the week.

And where was there for Kerry to hide? School? Her room?

Sometimes she thought she was happiest asleep, or remembering things. But then she had to come back to now, here, back to being the dead guy's sister.

She didn't mean to be cruel, she was just tired of it.

15

"Fourteen!" they screamed, and the train came around, disappearing into a papier-mâché tunnel. She took a sip of the shake to get the taste out of her mouth and stopped, cheeks still filled, getting her breath.

"If you don't feel good, stop," Coach offered, but Kerry shook her head.

She'd been drunk once, and this was how it felt—no control. She waited until a bubble of gas passed and started in again, trying to focus on something outside herself.

In the glass case beneath the register were two shelves of candy bars. A boy and a girl were bugging their mother to buy one. Just the thought of chocolate sickened her, the thick taste of it suffocating.

In her closet she had a cache of Hershey bars in her Doc Martens box, and a Milky Way in with her jewelry. She'd been good; she'd resisted them since Halloween. And when she did give in and gobble them down in the middle of some night, she promised she wouldn't replace them with anything.

Right. It all sounded good, she thought. But that's what she'd said the last time.

16

They cheered, and the manager came over to see how she was doing. The woman's record was seventeen, he said, by an FBI agent from Tyler, Texas.

Kerry turned the bun in her hands and concentrated. Her fingernails were dirty.

Matt had called her into his room. "Something's wrong," he said, and held out his hand.

She said she didn't see anything.

"Watch," he said, and took a pin from his corkboard. He pushed it into his fingertip. It stuck there, a drop of blood welling up.

"Oh, my God," Kerry said, "what are you doing?"

"I can't feel it," he said. "I can't feel any of them."

17

She laid her hand on her dad's, and he covered it.

"You know there is a chance," he said, "that he will get better."

And the way he said it, it was like she wanted him to die. Like, by not believing, she was killing him.

18

Even Stacey Gaither was cheering for her. She was officially the women's record holder; they'd put her name on the wall. Her and Scott Markham, a perfect pair. They could put a sign outside of town—Milesburg, Home of the Fat Man Champions.

She knew what her mother would say—the same thing she said when she dyed her hair with raspberry Kool-Aid, or when she'd gotten her nose pierced: "Why do you do these things to yourself?"

But see, her mom thought she already knew the answer.

19

She'd thrown up the first time she'd gotten drunk. She got Moriah's brother to buy her a pint of Southern Comfort and picked a Sunday afternoon to hike up to the cemetery. After visiting him she sat on a dead log and watched the river, tipping the sweet mouth of the bottle to hers. Below, sooty Milesburg filled the cold valley—the brick body shops and sad plazas—and she chose random cars and followed them through the empty streets.

She finished the bottle easily. It was only when she stood up to throw it that the liquor hit her. She bent over and coughed up her mom's lunch of kielbasa and beans, the crackers she'd hidden in her coat, the stolen after-dinner mints.

"Fuck you," she said, "just fuck all of you," and was surprised to find she was crying.

20

They brought a new plate. There was a crowd now. Families and old people, little kids standing on chairs. Everyone was cheering.

"Take your time," Coach said.

She had fifteen minutes, and she thought—for an instant—of eating all but one bite, just to spite them. They'd remember her better that way.

In the hospital Matt asked them not to take pictures of him. He sat propped up in bed, with tubes going up his nose. He had three IV lines; his arms were blue with bruises. After a chemo only their mom was allowed to see him, and she'd come back saying he was recovering, that maybe they could see him next week.

He got so thin he couldn't keep his rings on. Kerry had to tape them like Moriah's, and still they slid over his knuckles, fell ringing to the floor. His cheekbones poked out like a model's.

"You can have my CDs," he said. "Okay?"

21

"Twenty burgers!" the manager shouted, while Kerry was still trying to get it down. "Twenty burgers, the Fat Man says, and your entire bus eats for free!"

"The shake"—Moriah pointed—"you didn't finish it."

Kerry took a long pull and the straw slurped. It was funny; she didn't feel full. The applause didn't feel like anything.

She picked up another burger.

"That's twenty," Coach said. "You're all done."

Kerry shook her head.

"You're going to be sick."

Kerry just shrugged.

"You're so gross," Matt had said, watching her eat McDonald's. They were in the wagon, on the way to Gram's for Christmas. She was so hungry, and it was messy.

"God, what a pig. Use a napkin or something."

"Matthew!" their mom said.

"You know what they call her at school?"

"Matt, that's enough," their dad said.

"Free Willy."

"Shut up," Kerry said.

"And Shamu too."

"That's it," their mom said. "I don't want to hear another word out of your mouth."

22

It was easy. Only Coach was worried about her; the rest of them wanted to see her break the record.

Scott Markham and Matt were in the same class all the way through grade school. Matt used to do an impression of him. He flipped one eyelid inside out and popped spit bubbles with his mouth, cocked his head so it was resting on his shoulder.

"You're so pwetty," he said, and petted her arm like a dog, his fingers stiff.

"Stop," she said.

"I wuv you, Kewwy. I wuv you so much."

23

They'd have to put her name on top of his. Ten minutes left. The crowd went quiet with each bite, as if she might explode. It was stupid; she could eat ten more if she wanted to.

The night he died, no one told her. She was supposed to be asleep, but the phone woke her, and then she could hear her mom and dad talking, arguing, and then someone going out the door, the car backing down the drive.

Downstairs, someone opened and closed the fridge, then went into the TV room but didn't turn the set on. It was proof, she thought, and when the phone rang again, she stilled her breathing to hear what her dad said.

"Yes it is," he said. "Yes, I understand, thank you.

"She's already on her way.

"I appreciate it.

"Thank you again."

The next morning they came to her room, the two of them. She guessed they'd slept as little as she had. Her mom sat on her bed, her dad's hand on her shoulder. She had to understand, her mom said; sometimes there's nothing anyone can do.

For some reason Kerry laughed.

"Oh, baby," her mom said, and held her, as if she understood.

She had to get a new dress for the funeral because nothing fit, and they made her lay a rose on top of the coffin, a white one for innocence. She cried like she was supposed to, but in her room, with the door closed, she took a pin and scratched up all his Nirvana CDs so no one could ever play them again.

She pushed the last corner of the bun in, chewed, and swallowed.

"We have a new Fat Man record!" the manager said, and now Kerry leaned back in the chair and gave in to the crowd.

"Ker-ry, Ker-ry," the team chanted, and she thought that it really did work, that they'd win tonight and go on and take states. Stacey was clapping and bouncing up and down, so was Moriah. Even the old people were saying her name, the little kids, the truckers, everyone in the Fat Man. This was what it was like to be famous, she thought, to have everyone love you. It was dumb; none of them knew her at all, none of them understood anything. She wished they would just shut up.

"You okay there?" Coach asked, and Kerry shook her head no. "You feel like you're going to be sick?"

Yes, Kerry nodded, and stood up, her napkin falling to the carpet.

The manager took her arm and the crowd parted before her, still cheering. Her stomach surged and Kerry clamped a hand to her mouth. She could feel the solid heat of the burgers pushing up, insistent as lava.

The manager steered her to the women's room door and let go.

It was white inside, and brilliant, a kind of tiled heaven. She lunged for the first open stall she saw and doubled over her stomach. The toilet gaped up at her like an eye, a wide open mouth, expectant.

It came in a gush, splashing, plunking like stones dropped in water. She went to her knees on the cold floor and let it push out of her in bursts, flushing in between. It hurt her nose, fell to the bowl in bitter yellow strings. She was crying, out of sickness or for herself, she didn't know. Her mom and dad would never understand, she knew that. Why she did these things. Why she was so fucked up. She wanted to say she didn't hate him anymore, that she didn't love him, that none of it meant anything to her, though years later—a mother herself—she would see, would admit, finally, that of all the monuments she built to him, this would prove the most enduring, a record she was sure no one would ever break.

"You okay, miss?" [illegible] Kerry [illegible]. "What [illegible]" [illegible] wanted her to [illegible].

"Yes." Kerry nodded, and stood up, her napkin falling to the carpet.

The manager took her arm and she moved unsteadily between the tables, still clutching her stomach. [illegible] and Kerry clamped a hand to her mouth. She could feel the soup [illegible] the [illegible] posture up, [illegible] as level.

The manager steered her to the women's room. [illegible]

It was white tiled and bright. [illegible] and she lunged for the [illegible] stall. She saw the [illegible] over her stomach. The toilet paper [illegible]. The [illegible] a [illegible] mouth, expectant.

It came up in a rush, spinach, [illegible] like stones dropped in water. She went to her knees on the cold floor and [illegible] out of her [illegible], flushing [illegible]. It [illegible] her nose, fell to the bowl [illegible] yellow [illegible]. She was [illegible] for herself, [illegible] Her mom and dad [illegible] she knew. Why she did these things. Why she was so fucked up. She wanted to say she didn't [illegible] him anymore, that she didn't [illegible] him, that none of it meant anything to her. [illegible] she [illegible] herself. She would [illegible] that of all [illegible] would prove the [illegible] she [illegible] she would ever [illegible].

CONTRIBUTORS

John Barth is the author of twelve volumes of fiction and two essay collections. His awards include the National Book Award, the Lannan Foundation Lifetime Achievement Award, the F. Scott Fitzgerald Award, and the Pen/Malamud Short Story Award.

Thomas Beller is the author of *Seduction Theory,* a collection of stories, and editor of *Personals: Dreams and Nightmares from the Lives of 20 Young Writers.* His stories have appeared in numerous publications, including *Southwest Review, Ploughshares, The New Yorker,* and *Best American Short Stories.* His forthcoming novel, *Seconds of Pleasure,* will be published by Norton.

Jason Brown grew up in Maine and graduated from Bowdoin College in 1991. He received his MFA in writing from Cornell University in 1995, was a Wallace Stegner

Fellow and Truman Capote Fellow from 1996 to 1998, and is now a Jones Lecturer in Fiction at Stanford. His stories have appeared in *Best American Short Stories 1996* and *The Atlantic Monthly,* and his first collection, *Driving the Heart and Other Stories,* was published in April of this year.

Author of eighteen novels and five works of nonfiction, FREDERICK BUSCH is a recipient of the PEN/Malamud Award, the National Jewish Book Award, and the American Academy of Arts and Letters Fiction Award. He has been acting director of the Iowa Writer's Workshop and is currently the Edgar Fairchild Professor of Literature at Colgate University. His latest novel, *The Night Inspector,* was published this year.

ANDRE DUBUS was the author of numerous novels, short story and essay collections, including *Dancing After Hours* and *Meditations from a Movable Chair.* He was the recipient of the Rea Award for Short Fiction, the PEN/Malamud Award, and the American Academy of Arts and Letters Award.

BRIDGET ROHAN GARRITY attended the Iowa Writer's Workshop and is currently a Wallace Stegner Fellow at Stanford University.

TIM GAUTREAUX was born and raised in South Louisiana. His fiction has appeared in *The Atlantic Monthly,*

Harper's, GQ, Story, New Stories from the South, Best American Short Stories, and in his first book, *Same Place, Same Things.* His novel, *Welding with Children,* was published this year. He is a professor of creative writing at South Louisiana University.

Mary Gordon is the author of *The Company of Women, The Rest of Life,* and *The Other Side* as well as the critically acclaimed memoir *The Shadow Man.* Winner of the Lila Acheson Wallace Reader's Digest Writer's Award, a Guggenheim Fellowship, and the 1996 O. Henry Prize for best short story, she teaches at Barnard College and lives in New York City.

Ralph Lombreglia is the author of two story collections, *Men Under Water* and *Make Me Work.* His work has appeared regularly in *The Atlantic Monthly* and *The New Yorker,* among other magazines, and in such anthologies as *Best American Short Stories, The Vintage Book of Contemporary American Short Stories,* and *The O. Henry Awards.* A former Stegner Fellow at Stanford University, he now lives in the Boston area with his wife and daughter and teaches at Boston University. "Cashmere Christmas" is adapted from a novel-in-progress for which he has received a Guggenheim Fellowship and a Whiting Writer's Award.

Barry Lopez is the author of four works of nonfiction, including *Arctic Dreams* and *Of Wolves and Men;* seven works of fiction, including *Field Notes* and *Winter Count;* and a novella-length fable, *Crow and Weasel.* His work regularly appears in *Harper's,* where he is a contributing editor, as well as in *The Paris Review, Orion, The Georgia Review,* and elsewhere. The recipient of numerous literary awards, including the National Book Award for nonfiction, he lives in western Oregon. "Stolen Horses" is excerpted from his forthcoming novel, *Light Action in the Caribbean*, to be published by Knopf this summer.

JACOB MOLYNEUX grew up near Boston, graduated from Oberlin College, and received an MFA from the University of North Carolina—Greensboro. He has been a writing fellow at the Fine Arts Work Center in Provincetown, and held Wallace Stegner and Truman Capote fellowships at Stanford University, where he is currently a lecturer in fiction.

JOYCE CAROL OATES's most recent novel is *Broke Heart Blues,* and her most recent short story collection is *The Collector of Hearts.* She is a professor of humanities at Princeton University.

CHRIS OFFUTT is the author two books of short stories, *Kentucky Strait* and *Out of the Woods.* He has also published a novel, *The Good Brother,* and a memoir, *The Same River Twice.* His work is widely anthologized and has been translated into several languages. His writing has received many honors, including a Whiting Award, a Guggenheim Fellowship, an award from the American Academy of Arts and Letters, and a fellowship from the National Endowment for the Arts. He is a native of eastern Kentucky, where he now lives with his wife and sons. He teaches at Morehead State University.

STEWART O'NAN was born and raised in Pittsburgh. His short story collection, *In the Walled City,* won the Drue Heinz Prize, and his first novel, *Snow Angels,* led *Granta* to include him on their list of the 20 Best Young American Novelists. Since then he's won awards for *The Names of the Dead, The Speed Queen,* and *A World Away.* His latest novel is *A Prayer for the Dying.*

JIM SHEPARD is the author of the novels *Flights, Paper Doll, Lights Out in the Reptile House, Kiss of the Wolf,* and *Nosferatu.* His stories have appeared in *The New Yorker, Harper's, The Atlantic Monthly, Esquire, TriQuarterly, The Paris Review,* and *Best American Short Stories. Batting Against Castro,* a collection of stories published in 1996, was described as "a masterpiece" by *The New York Times.*

TOBIAS WOLFF's books include the memoirs *This Boy's Life* and *In Pharaoh's Army;* the short novel *The Barracks Thief;* and three collections of stories, *In the Garden of the North American Martyrs, Back in the World,* and, most recently, *The Night in Question.* He has also edited several anthologies, among them *Best American Short Stories 1994, A Doctor's Visit: The Short Stories of Anton Chekhov,* and

The Vintage Book of Contemporary American Short Stories. His work has been translated widely and has received numerous awards, including the PEN-Faulkner Award, the *Los Angeles Times* Book Award, and the Rea Award for the Short Story. He teaches at Stanford University.